## COMMAND PERFORMANCE

When the wealthy Lord Linton offered to provide
Jessica with a London townhouse and a lavish
allowance, it was understood by both of them
what he wanted from her.

But now as Jessica stood before him in her
creamy white negligee and saw the approving
glint in his eyes and his slow, lazy smile of
anticipation, she realized how hard it would be
for her to give him a proper return on his
investment. For Linton clearly expected her to be
a lady wise in the ways of sensual love, and she
was as lacking in experience as she was trembling
in trepidation.

Linton was going to get less than he counted on
—and more than he bargained for. . . .

# HIS LORDSHIP'S MISTRESS

# HIS LORDSHIP'S MISTRESS

## JOAN WOLF

A SIGNET BOOK

**NEW AMERICAN LIBRARY**

TIMES MIRROR

Copyright © 1982 by Joan Wolf

SIGNET TRADEMARK REG. U.S. PAT. OFF. AND FOREIGN COUNTRIES
REGISTERED TRADEMARK—MARCA REGISTRADA
HECHO EN CHICAGO, U.S.A.

SIGNET, SIGNET CLASSICS, MENTOR, PLUME, MERIDIAN AND NAL
BOOKS are published by The New American Library, Inc.,
1633 Broadway, New York, New York 10019

First Printing, April, 1982

1  2  3  4  5  6  7  8  9

PRINTED IN THE UNITED STATES OF AMERICA

## PUBLISHER'S NOTE

# Chapter One

But keep the wolf far thence...
                        —JOHN WEBSTER

Two weeks after her stepfather was buried, Jessica Andover sat in the mellow, panelled library of Winchcombe listening to her lawyer detail the state of her affairs. They were not good. In fact, they were disastrous.

"It is in the highest degree unfortunate that your father did not secure the estate directly to you, Jessica my dear," Mr. Samuel Grassington said sadly. "However, he was a young and vigorous man when he died. He could not be made to see the importance of settling his affairs, and without the proper safeguards your property was at the free disposal of your mother's second husband."

Jessica's lips tightened. "I know that all too well, Mr. Grassington."

Mr. Grassington cleared his throat. He had been an uncomfortable spectator at one of Jessica's confrontations with Sir Thomas Lissett. "Ah, yes," he said.

"How much did my stepfather squeeze the estate for, Mr. Grassington? The horses, the card games, and the women must have cost a pretty penny I should imagine."

The old lawyer looked unhappy. "I wish they were the whole of it, my dear."

Her gray eyes darkened. "What do you mean?"

"It has become regrettably clear that Sir Thomas Lissett made a great number of unwise investments."

"With my money?"

"With your money."

Jessica fixed the lawyer with somber eyes. "What is the total debt?"

"Considering that Sir Thomas has not been dead three weeks and that all the creditors have not yet applied to me . . ."

"How much?" Jessica repeated steadily.

He told her.

There was a stunned silence. "It is worse than I thought," she finally said quietly.

"It is not good, my dear. I am so very sorry."

Jessica sat for a minute with bent head; then she looked up. "What about the boys?" she asked stiffly.

"I had more success with your stepfather about making a will than I had with your father. He could not name you as guardian of your half brothers as you are not yet twenty-one, so I persuaded Sir Thomas to name me the legal guardian of all three of you."

Warm color flushed into Jessica Andover's cheeks. "Thank you, Mr. Grassington. I could not have borne it if . . ." She stopped and bit her lip, emotion for the moment overcoming the cool composure she usually presented to the world.

"Needless to say, I have no intention of interfering with how you rear Geoffrey and Adrian. You have had them in charge since the death of your mother and you seem to be succeeding admirably." The elderly man reached across the table, and in an uncharacteristic gesture of affection covered her hand. "I only wish I could have done more, my dear. But there was no way I could stop him from running through your property."

"I know." She raised her chin in a gesture only too familiar to Mr. Grassington. "My situation then is this. I have myself and my two brothers to support. Adrian is to start Eton this year and the money must be found to send him. Money must also be found to pay Geoffrey's tuition for his remaining five years at Eton. I don't think Geoffrey is at all interested in going to the university, but Adrian must certainly go to Cambridge. You tell me the farms are all heavily mortgaged and I cannot afford to redeem them. They must be sold, then. The money will help to pay off some of the debt. The loss of the farms leaves me bereft of regular income, however."

"Tuition is very expensive," murmured Mr. Grassington.

"I know." Jessica's voice was very firm. "I shall have to make money out of the horses."

"The horses? Of course you will have to sell the horses, Jessica."

"I have no intention of selling the horses," she returned. "Didn't I just say I needed a regular income?"

"I don't understand what you mean. How are you going to get a regular income out of the horses?"

"My stepfather spent a great deal of money on those horses, Mr. Grassington, and whatever his faults, he knew horseflesh. I have the makings of a

3

very impressive little stud at Winchcombe. A very profitable little stud, I might add, if it is handled properly."

"But my dear . . ." the old lawyer protested faintly.

Jessica's gray eyes were burning with intensity. "You live in Cheltenham, Mr. Grassington. You can't be unaware of the amount of money that a wealthy owner will pay for a good race horse. I plan to breed good race horses and collect some of that money. I have the initial investment sitting right in my own stableyard, eating their heads off. I'd be a fool not to take advantage of it."

"Are you serious, Jessica?"

"Deadly serious, sir. I have very few talents, but I do know horses. And I'm not afraid of work."

Mr. Grassington looked very uneasy. "Jessica, my dear, there is no need for you to turn yourself into a stableboy. There are certainly other ways of dealing with this problem."

"I should be very happy if you would tell me what they are."

Mr. Grassington cleared his throat. "You are an extremely attractive young woman," he said finally, "You come from one of the best families in the county. There are many men, men of substance, who would be pleased to marry you if only you would give them a chance."

She stared for a minute at the kind, concerned face of the old lawyer who had known her since her birth, then abruptly turned away toward the window. "No," said Jessica, directly, firmly, and finally.

"Why not?" he persisted.

The girl gazed steadily out the window, her profile aloof and withdrawn. "That was my mother's solution, if you remember," she said evenly. "The burden of running an estate was too much for her, so she married again to have someone to take the burden off her shoulders." She turned now to face the lawyer, and passion burned in her clear gray eyes. "Do you really think, having just gotten out from under the yoke of my stepfather's greed, that I am going to turn my property and my person over to some *other* man?"

"Jessica! All men are not like your stepfather."

"I know that," she replied steadily. "But I have no intention of marrying, Mr. Grassington. I am perfectly capable of taking care of myself and of my brothers."

"Selling off the farms will cover only a part of Sir Thomas's debt," he reminded her gently.

"So I see. I had hoped I wouldn't have to do this," said Jessica, "but I shall have to mortgage Winchcombe."

Mr. Grassington sat frowning at the table for almost a full minute; then he spoke slowly. "I think perhaps Sir Edmund Belton would help you. He was a friend of your father's. I should feel comfortable knowing that he was the one who held the mortgage on Winchcombe."

Jessica nodded thoughtfully. "Yes, that is a good idea. I'll go to see him tomorrow."

The lawyer began putting his papers away. He looked up at last and said, "Are you sure this is what you want to do?"

"Yes."

A rueful smile crossed the old man's face as he

looked at the determined face of the girl he had been trying to advise. "You are just like your grandfather," he said.

She gave him her rare smile. "I take that as a compliment."

He picked up her hand and kissed it with old-fashioned courtesy. "It is, my dear. It is."

Sir Edmund Belton was more than pleased to be able to help Jessica. He was a man of fifty or so, but since the death of his only son in the Peninsula he had aged twenty years. He assured her he would be happy to advance her whatever sum she needed. He did not even want to hold a mortgage in return, but Jessica insisted. After they had decided to put the whole transaction into the hands of their respective lawyers, they sat drinking tea and chatting comfortably in Sir Edmund's old-fashioned drawing room. One of the pleasures Sir Edmund found in talking to Jessica was that he never had to ask her to repeat herself. He was rather hard of hearing, a defect he hated to admit to. He often had to strain to hear a speaker, but as he became intensely annoyed if someone shouted at him, his conversational partners often found themselves in a quandary. Not Jessica. She had a superbly deep, clear voice which she could pitch effortlessly to Sir Edmund's hearing level without seeming to shout at all.

She was rising to take her leave when the door opened and a tall, dark man came into the room. "Oh, there you are, Harry," said Sir Edmund. "I want you to meet my nephew, Jessica. Captain Henry Belton.

This is Miss Jessica Andover of Winchcombe, Harry."

Jessica gazed steadily at the dark, rather hard face of Harry Belton. He was, she knew, heir to Melford Hall now that Sir Edmund's son John was dead. "How do you do," she said, and held out her hand.

Captain Belton took it slowly, his own eyes intent on Jessica. He saw a tall, slim girl of striking appearance. Her face was thin, with beautiful, translucent skin and long, finely drawn features. Her brows and lashes were dark, but the large eyes were pale gray and very clear, like water. Her thick hair, which was braided in a coronet on top of her head, was brown, but there was a shade of tawny autumn leaf in it, a color indescribable and one he had never seen before. "I am very pleased to meet you, Miss Andover," he said, 'and held her hand for a moment too long.

"Are you making a long stay, Captain?" Jessica asked, recovering her hand.

"I am afraid not," he said regretfully. "My regiment is going to Ireland, unfortunately. I shall be here only a week or so."

"Well, perhaps we shall see more of you at some future time," she said, dismissing him from her thoughts. "I must be going now, Sir Edmund. I cannot thank you sufficiently. I think you know what it means to me."

"My dear girl, I am happy to be able to help. You know how fond of you I am. Come again and see me soon."

Jessica leaned forward and kissed him lightly on the cheek. "I will," she said. She directed a brief smile at Captain Belton and was gone.

The captain stood looking after her before he turned to his uncle. "What was that all about?" he asked in tones that had been trained on the parade ground.

"There's no need to shout, Harry," Sir Edmund replied crossly. "The poor girl has found herself in the devil of a fix, that's all. That scoundrel Sir Thomas Lissett has gone and gotten himself killed and left her with two young boys and a mountain of debt. I just told her I'd hold a mortgage on Winchcombe."

There was a very intent look in Captain Belton's brown eyes. "I thought Winchcombe belonged to the Andovers. Surely Lissett couldn't touch the estate."

"He could and he did," Sir Edmund replied shortly. "Pity he didn't get killed sooner."

"How did he die?"

"Hunting accident."

"I see. And you are going to hold a mortgage on Winchcombe so Miss Andover can pay her stepfather's debts?"

"Yes."

"How very interesting," said Captain Henry Belton softly.

# Chapter Two

Trust not therefore the outward show;
           —THOMAS RICHARDSON

It was a beautiful early August day almost a year later when Sir Henry Belton, owner for two months now of Melton Hall, drove his grays up the drive of Jessica Andover's home. His dark eyes rested appreciatively on the mellow pink brick of Winchcombe, which was looking at its best against the dark green foliage of the surrounding park. It was not a great mansion; it had been built by a seventeenth-century Andover as a comfortable, easy-going gentleman's house, and it still retained that look. When Sir Henry inquired for Miss Andover at the door he was informed that she was down at the stables, so he turned his horses into a wide, shaded, avenue at the side of the house.

The first person he saw when he pulled into the stableyard was Adrian Lissett, Jessica's youngest brother. "How do you do, Sir Henry," he said, politely coming over to the phaeton. "Are you looking for my sister?"

As Adrian was holding his horses for him, Sir Henry got down from the phaeton. "Jem!" the boy called, and a stableboy came running. "Take Sir

9

Henry's horses, will you?" Adrian asked, and then turned to look inquiringly at the man standing next to him. The younger Lissett was a slim boy of ten with brown eyes, shining brown hair, and a tan that showed he had spent his summer vacation for the most part out of doors. He was dressed in well-worn riding breeches and his shirt sleeves were rolled up.

"Yes," Sir Henry replied in his clipped, military voice. "They told me at the house that Miss Andover was down here."

"She's working Northern Light down in the paddock." Adrian fell into step beside him as he walked past the stable block and headed toward the paddock area. Geoffrey, two years older than Adrian and more broadly built, was sitting on top of the paddock gate. Standing next to him was a towheaded stableboy. Both boys turned at the sound of Adrian's voice.

"Jess has got him going like a lamb," Geoffrey informed his brother. "He's a beauty!" he added with enthusiasm. Then, a definite afterthought, "How do you do, sir."

Sir Henry nodded, and all four of them turned to look at the horse and rider in the paddock. But Jessica had seen them and called "Geoff, that's enough for today, I think. Take him back to the stable for me."

The boy jumped with alacrity to do her bidding, and Jessica dismounted and came over to Sir Henry Belton. "He's going to be a marvel," she said easily. "Riding him is like sitting on a keg of dynamite." Like her brothers she was dressed in boots and breeches and her hair fell in a thick braid down between her shoulders.

"I hate to see you working yourself like that," Sir Henry said in his abrupt way.

A faint frown appeared between Jessica's dark brows. She didn't consider that he had any right at all to comment upon her welfare, but it had become her policy to be as pleasant to him as possible, and she returned a noncommittal answer.

"I am leaving tomorrow for Lancashire," he said, "and before I go I should like an opportunity to speak to you privately."

Her narrow nostrils quivered slightly, but she replied calmly enough. "Certainly. We'll go up to the house if you like."

"Thank you," he said crisply, and the two of them turned up the path he had driven down only a short time earlier.

Jessica was very quiet at dinner that evening. Dining at Winchcombe was a highly informal affair. Gathered around the table in the faded blue dining room were Jessica, Geoffrey, Adrian, and Miss Sarah Burnley, Jessica's onetime governess, who now spent her time running the house, as Jessica was fully occupied by the stables.

Miss Burnley had been engaged by Mr. Christopher Andover seventeen years ago to instruct his daughter and had been at Winchcombe ever since. Her credentials as governess were somewhat limited, for she did not know Italian, painted very poorly, and had extremely strange ideas about geography. She had once solemnly assured Jessica that Tripoli was in the Southern Hemisphere. What she did have, however, was a beautiful speaking voice, and Mr. Andover, who prized good speech above all else, had engaged her on the strength of that. She had been successful in training Jessica's voice to reach her own high standards. She had also imparted to her young charge her profound enthusiasm for the plays of William Shakespeare. Many long winter afternoons had been spent in the schoolroom of Winchcombe reading aloud—"with *feeling*, Jessica dear"—from the plays of the great bard.

Now she looked at Jessica's abstracted face and asked gently, "I hope Sir Henry did not bring bad news this afternoon, Jessica?"

"Not precisely," said Jessica in the cool voice that told them all she did not want to discuss it.

"Perhaps he wants to buy Northern Light," Adrian said around a mouthful of beef pie.

"Don't talk with your mouth full, Adrian," his sister said automatically. "He is not interested in Northern Light and even if he were it would do him no good. Northern Light is not for sale."

"Of course he isn't!" Geoffrey put in indignantly. "Northern Light is the best two-year-old in the country. He is sure to win all the major races next year. Why, there isn't enough money in the world to buy Northern Light!"

Jessica smiled at Geoffrey, then turned to Miss Burnley, who was saying, a pucker between her thin brows. "But Jessica, I didn't know you were going to *race* horses. I thought you were just going to sell them."

"One must demonstrate the value of one's horses, Burnie, before one can sell them," Jessica replied, helping herself to some more beef pie. The physically active life she was leading always left her ravenously hungry by dinner time. "If Northern Light does as well as we hope," she explained to the puzzled face of her governess, "he will command enormous fees when we retire him to stud. And the stud fees are what are going to pay our bills in the future."

Miss Burnley put down her fork. " 'A horse, a horse, my kingdom for a horse!' " she quoted thrillingly, and Geoffrey and Adrian exchanged long-suffering looks. It was a quotation they were overfamiliar with.

"Now, Burnie, don't get started on that fellow Kean again," Geoffrey said hastily. "Ever since you and Jess saw him in Cheltenham last week you have been talking about nothing else."

"And *your* conversation, my dear Geoffrey," said Miss Burnley with gentle dignity, "is somewhat limited as well."

Adrian grinned. "Burnie's right, Geoff. All you ever talk about is horses."

"If you boys had accompanied us to the performance of *Richard III* you would have found yourselves as much in awe as Jessica and I. Such power. Such feeling."

Geoffrey opened his mouth to reply, then met his

sister's eyes. Resolutely he shut his lips and applied himself to his plate. Serenely, Miss Burnley continued. "I understand from my cousin in London that Covent Garden stood half empty all last season. Mr. Kemble is, of course, a well-known actor, but if Covent Garden is to compete with Drury Lane the management will have to find an actor to rival Mr. Kean. And that," she sighed nostalgically, "will be very difficult."

Jessica was staring at her, an arrested look in her gray eyes. "How much money do you think Mr. Kean makes, Burnie?" she asked.

"I don't know what his salary is, my dear, but I'm sure he gets bonuses. He received several hundred pounds for that one performance in Cheltenham. I know that from Mr. Francis, the manager of the Cheltenham Theatre."

"Oh," said Jessica, frowning thoughtfully.

"Are you going to see that mare of Redgate's tomorrow?" Geoffrey asked his sister after a suitable pause had assured him that the topic of Edmund Kean was concluded.

"No," she returned. "I am going into Cheltenham to see Mr. Grassington."

"May I come with you?" asked Adrian, who never missed an opportunity to visit Dr. Morrow, their physician. Adrian was fascinated by medicine.

"Of course," his sister assured him. Adrian, she knew, would be closeted with his idol for the morning and she would be free to consult privately with Mr. Grassington.

Geoffrey and Miss Burnley exchanged glances, but neither said anything further. They knew that look on Jessica's face and knew that further questions would be pointless. If something were up they would have to wait until she chose to tell them.

Mr. Grassington knew that look also. He asked her to sit down and gazed worriedly at the remote, austere face of the girl he held in such affection. "How can I help you, my dear?" he asked quietly.

She came directly to the point. "What are the terms of the mortgage on Winchcombe? Does it run for a specified period of time or can it be called in at any time?"

Mr. Grassington looked appalled. "You don't mean Sir Henry has asked you for the money?"

Her mouth, which was peculiarly expressive, looked very firm. "What are the terms of the mortgage?" she asked again.

"Mr. Canning, Sir Edmund's lawyer, drew it up," he said. "He naturally wrote it in favor of the holder."

"Do you mean he can call it in any time he chooses?"

"He must give you two months' notice," he replied, his mouth very dry. "Jessica, my dear, what has happened?"

There was no flicker of expression on her face. What she thought, what she felt, she had long since learned to keep to herself. Ever since her mother had died ten years ago she had stood on her own feet. She was aware of the sympathy on the old man's face but instinctively she shied away from it. She could not afford it. It would weaken her. So she said now in a calm, self-possessed voice, "Sir Henry wants to marry me. If I do not agree to his extremely distasteful proposal, he intimates that he will foreclose on my mortgage."

"He could not mean that, Jessica! Why, such behavior is, well, blackmail."

Jessica's lips twisted contemptuously. "He meant it. It is just the sort of thing a man of his stamp would resort to."

Mr. Grassington nervously shuffled some papers on his desk. "I did not know that Sir Henry had ever been over to Winchcombe," he said tentatively.

"He has been coming regularly this past month," she replied. "I thought he was interested in the horses. It now appears he was interested in the whole property."

"*Or* the property's owner," put in Mr. Grassington meaningfully.

Jessica looked scornful. "Oh, he made me a ridiculous speech about how he had decided to marry me a year ago when first he met me at Melford Hall. It's more likely that he decided then to acquire Winchcombe. It would set fewer people's backs up if he did it by marrying me, but I am not going to oblige him."

"Is it so difficult for you to believe that a man might want you for yourself?" the old lawyer asked gently.

Her dark brows rose. "He has gone about demonstrating that in rather an odd fashion."

"Yes. Sir Henry is a crude man, I fear. But, Jessica, I do not think his interest is Winchcombe." He paused. "Do you possibly think you might consider marrying him?"

"No."

"But to lose Winchcombe—and after you have worked so hard, my dear!" He looked in distress at her thin face—too thin, he thought. She was wearing herself out. The beautiful white and rose of her skin had turned a pale golden brown from the sun. He shook his head mournfully. "What else can you do?" he asked.

"If I marry Sir Henry I lose Winchcombe anyway," said Jessica. "A married woman has little say over her own property. No, as I told you once before, I have no intention of making the same mistake my mother did. I will manage by myself."

"But how?"

"I will pay Sir Henry the mortgage money."

"I do not see how you can get it. If I had it I would give it to you, you must know that. But I do not have it."

She smiled at him. "You are very kind, Mr. Grassington, and I thank you." She rose, and the smile died away, to be replaced by a look so intense it seemed to burn through him. "I will get that money if it kills me," she said in a taut, determined voice. "No one is going to take Winchcombe away from me."

"Oh my dear," he said helplessly.

"No one," she repeated fiercely, and her eyes looked almost silver in her suddenly pale face. She turned on her heel and left the room with swift grace.

The old lawyer stared after her with worried eyes. When Jessica was angry she was capable of anything. And from the look on her face he knew that she was very angry indeed.

# Chapter Three

Give money me; take friendship whoso list!
　　　　　　　　　—BARNABY GOOGE

Three days later Jessica set out for London, accompanied by Miss Burnley. She paid a visit to Clarges Street, where she arranged to borrow money at a depressingly high interest rate from Mr. King, a well-known moneylender. The money from Mr. King she would use to pay off Sir Henry Belton. Unfortunately, the only collateral she had to offer Mr. King was a mortgage on Winchcombe. Jessica then spent a week at Stevens' Hotel; during that time, unknown to Miss Burnley, she paid another visit, this one to Mr. Harris, the manager of the Covent Garden Theatre.

Jessica had six months to pay back Mr. King, and she had every intention of doing so. After many hours of deep thought she had determined a course of action for herself. It was not an easy decision for her to make, but she did not have many options. Marry for money she would not do. The thought of putting herself into the power of some man for the rest of her life filled her with horror. She might as well sell herself, she thought.

Which had brought her to her second option. She knew the amount of money her stepfather had spent on women. It appeared, she thought grimly to herself, that there was a good chance of making money by selling oneself temporarily. If anyone two years ago had told her she would consider becoming some rich man's mistress she would have stared incredulously. But in her present situation she didn't see any other way out. The world would condemn such a course of action, she knew. But then she had no intention of letting her world know what she had done. And Jessica, who had highly ethical but unusual standards, found the idea less distasteful than swearing to love, honor, and obey someone she hated and despised.

Simply stated, she had two boys who had to be put through school, and a mortgage on her only means of income. If she lost Winchcombe there would be no Eton, no Cambridge, no future for her brothers. Or for Miss Burnley. Or for her either if she steadfastly refused to marry. She was not even qualified to be a governess. The only solution was to clear Winchcombe of debt and go back to raising horses. Before she and Miss Burnley left for London Jessica had made up her mind, and when her mind was made up an earthquake would not move her.

In September Adrian and Geoffrey left for school. After they had left, Jessica received an urgent message from a distant cousin in Scotland. The cousin was very ill and wanted to see Jessica.

"I never heard of this Jean Cameron!" protested Miss Burnley.

"I have," Jessica replied ressuringly. "My mother was Scottish, you know, even if she was born and raised in France. My grandfather fought at Culloden and consequently had to flee the country. He joined the French army and married another Scottish exile. My mother was their only child. This Jean Cameron is the daughter of my grandfather's first cousin. She is quite elderly now and apparently rather wealthy. She says something about making 'restitution' to my grandfather's only grandchild for all he suffered for the 'cause.' " Jessica looked up from the letter she was holding. She knew it by heart, since she had written it herself. "It sounds as though she is thinking of leaving me some money, Burnie. God knows we could use it. I'd better go."

Miss Burnley had finally agreed and Jessica had packed her bags. She told Miss Burnley that Cousin Jean had arranged for a boat to take her from Dover to Perth, and she persuaded her old governess that she did not need any escort. "A friend of Cousin Jean's will be waiting for me when I arrive in London," she said glibly. "I shall be well taken care of, Burnie. You are needed here." After overcoming Miss Burnley's objections Jessica wrote a letter to her brothers giving them the same information she had imparted to the governess. She also wrote to Mr. Grassington. On September 16 she set out for London.

The place she went first after settling into the inexpensive lodging she had found during her week's sojourn in London with Miss Burnley was Covent Garden Theatre. Men looked for mistresses who were actresses or opera dancers, so Jessica's limited worldly wisdom told her. She couldn't be an opera dancer to save her soul, but she had, thanks to Miss Burnley, a well-trained speaking voice. She thought she could act. Apparently Mr. Harris had thought so too, for he had engaged to hire her a month ago.

Covent Garden was in trouble and none knew it better than Thomas Harris. The famous classical actor John Kemble and his equally talented sister Mrs. Siddons had been the mainstays of the theatre for years. But Mrs. Siddons was retired now and Kemble had given up most of his roles to Charles Mayne Young. Young was a tall, good-looking man with a melodious voice he used to good effect, but he could not vie with Edmund Kean. All of last season Kean had packed Drury Lane with his magnetic, naturalistic acting. Clearly the classical style of acting so nobly embodied in Kemble and Young was on the wane. Thomas Harris realized quite well that Kemble now was not an adequate draw and that it would be madness to allow Covent Garden to remain exclusively the home of classical acting. He needed someone who could compete with Kean. And then a young girl who called herself Jessica O'Neill arrived. She told him she was an actress who had previously only worked in small playhouses in the west of Ireland, and he gave her an audition.

He had been immediately taken by her marvelous voice. There was also a distinction about her that he thought would go over well with a London audience. He liked the way she held her head, so erect and beautifully balanced. He was struck by the cool, shining look of her large eyes. She looked as if she had the habit, founded on experience, of not being afraid of

/

anything. She had read the trial scene from *The Merchant of Venice* for him and her rendering of Portia had power and authority, yet was at the same time unmistakably feminine.

Harris had no intention of mounting a production of *The Merchant of Venice*. Kean's Shylock was justly famous, and however good a Portia he presented, Harris knew he could not avoid unfavorable comparisons to Drury Lane. What he wanted was to present an actor—or actress—who embodied the same style of acting as Kean, romantic and naturalistic, in a new role, and preferably one unsuited to the talents of the Drury Lane star. The day Jessica presented herself at Covent Garden to begin work Harris had her read Juliet. The next day he put her on the stage and had her do the balcony scene with Charles Mayne Young. The result was even better than he had dreamed; he had his new star.

Jessica was somewhat bewildered at finding herself taken so seriously by the Covent Garden management. She had hoped merely for a small part, one that would give her the kind of exposure she needed to accomplish her purpose. She was not sure she wanted to be a star on the scale Mr. Harris was envisioning, but as the weeks went by and rehearsals intensified she found herself caught up in the production and, most of all, in the role.

She had enormous sympathy for Juliet. Romantic love was something Jessica was unfamiliar with, but the intensity of Juliet's feeling was something she could understand. Wasn't she herself prepared to venture into a strange and alien world for the sake of two

23

young brothers whom she loved? And Juliet's terrible isolation as the play moved toward its conclusion was frighteningly familiar to Jessica. When she stood before the friar, deserted by father, mother, and nurse, Juliet's words seemed to come from within her own deepest self:

> O' bid me leap, rather than marry Paris,
> From off the battlements of yonder tower,
> Or walk in thievish ways, or bid me lurk
> Where serpents are; chain me with roaring bears,
> Or shut me nightly in a charnel house,
> O'ercovered quite with dead men's rattling bones,
> With reeky shanks and yellow chapless skulls;
> Or bid me go into a new-made grave
> And hide me with a dead man in his shroud—
> Things that, to hear them told, have made me tremble—
> And I will do it without fear or doubt ...

They were Jessica's exact feelings about marriage with Sir Henry Belton.

The Covent Garden management was delighted with Jessica and raised her salary to twenty pounds a week. All during the weeks of rehearsals rumors of her beauty and genius were skillfully spread throughout London. *Romeo and Juliet* was to open on October 6, and by early that afternoon the various entrances to Covent Garden Theatre were surrounded by crowds eager to obtain admission. When the doors opened at half-past five an immense throng poured into the house and rushed into the pit and galleries. Before long the boxes and circles were filled with the most famous men and women of the age, all eager to see Jessica O'Neill, the "new Siddons."

Jessica stood in the Green Room frozen into immobility. When she was called to the stage she stood in the wings certain she would not be able to utter a word. She heard Mrs. Brereton, who was playing the nurse say, "Where's this girl? What, Juliet!" and, taking a deep breath, she walked on stage.

# Chapter Four

He was . . . to each well-thinking mind
A spotless friend, a matchless man,
whose virtue ever shined.
                    —FULKE GREVILLE

London could talk of nothing but Jessica O'Neill.
When the curtain had fallen on her first performance
the audience had burst into a wild tumult of applause.
The management had announced a new play for the
following evening, but hundreds of voices had shouted
back, demanding another performance of *Romeo and
Juliet*. The manager had yielded, and *Romeo and
Juliet* ran the next night as well.

The critics were universally enthusiastic. The
*Morning Chronicle* wrote, "It was not altogether the
matchless beauty of form and face, but the spirit of
perfect innocence and purity that seemed to glisten in
her speaking eyes, and breathe from her chiselled
lips." The *Morning Post* raved, "A sense of innate delicacy, of rare sensibility glowing through the fervour
of her words, and the presence of passion and growing
strength, rendered her performance a delight to be-
hold." And William Hazlitt, writing for the *Cham-
pion*, thought "she perfectly conceived what would be
generally felt by the female mind in the extraordinary

and overpowering situations in which she was placed." Crowds were turned away from the theatre each night she played. Jessica, to her own astonishment, was famous.

Philip Romney, Earl of Linton, came to London near the middle of October to find the town still in an uproar over Jessica O'Neill. The Romneys belonged to that select group of families who had virtually ruled England during much of the seventeenth and eighteenth centuries. Together with the great Whig houses of Cavendish, Russell, Grenville, and Spenser, they owned vast numbers of acres and were born to an almost automatic right to a voice in the government and a seat in the cabinet. And of all the great landowning Whig aristocrats none looked more the part than did the present Earl of Linton. He was at this time twenty-seven years of age and possessed a personal presence that instantly suggested a prince in very truth, a ruler, warrior, and patron. Ironically, he was not involved with government, the Whigs having been out of power for many years, but he was interested in certain areas of social reform and made it a point to be in the House whenever one of his causes came up for a vote. He spent the greater part of the year in Kent on his principal estate of Staplehurst.

He had come up to town because his elder sister and her children had arrived at Staplehurst for a prolonged visit with his mother and he had long ago decided that a little of Maria's company was more than sufficient. She was ten years his senior and tended to dwell at great length on the fact that as the only son of the family it was his duty to get married. He knew very well that it was his duty and he had every intention of fulfilling it—some day. In the meanwhile he did not relish Maria's strictures and he did not want to upset his mother by quarrelling with his determined sister, so he decided that it would be a good idea for him to pay a visit to London.

His many friends were delighted to see him, and it wasn't long before Lord George Litcham invited him to share Lord George's sister's box at Covent Garden. "You really must see Miss O'Neill, Philip," he said. "She has quite stolen Kean's thunder, you know."

"Well, if she is half as good as Kean she is worth seeing," Linton replied good-naturedly. "I saw him as Shylock last year and I still haven't forgotten the impression he produced. Like a chapter of Genesis, I thought."

"She is every bit as good. And infinitely more beautiful."

"Oh?" Linton raised an inquiring eyebrow.

Lord George smiled briefly. "After her performances the Green Room is so filled with her admirers that one is fortunate to get two words with her."

Linton looked amused. "Then certainly I must see her, George. Thank Lady Wetherby for me and say I shall be happy to make one of her party tomorrow evening."

Lady Wetherby's box was very near the stage, and Linton had an excellent view of Jessica's performance. He had rather thought he had outgrown *Romeo and*

*Juliet* and was surprised and then deeply moved by the swift and tragic beauty of the story as it unfolded before him. Jessica's beautiful voice, clearly audible in the farthest reaches of the gallery, gave such an intensity of feeling to the poetry that lines that had hitherto seemed outrageous now appeared glorious expressions of the truth and ardor of young love. And she was indeed striking, with that magnificent skin, that mouth with the curve that could be so tender yet so resolute, the arch of those dark eyebrows with the wonderful gray eyes beneath them.

"I'd like to meet Miss O'Neill," he said to Lord George after the performance was over.

"Oh Lord, Philip, I hope *you* aren't going to enter the sweepstake for her favors," said Lord George.

"Is there a sweepstake?"

"Assuredly. The betting at the clubs is in favor of Ashford at the moment. He is the richest one of the lot."

"A high flyer, I see."

"Oh, definitely."

They had entered the Green Room by now, and it was indeed thronged with the great and the famous. Jessica was standing with her back to the full-length mirror talking to Lord Debenham. "Can you introduce me, George?" Linton asked softly.

"Come along," replied his friend, and prepared to shoulder his way through the crowd. But it was not necessary. People naturally stepped aside for Philip Romney; it was his fine unconscious way, his friend thought ruefully, of outshining, overlooking, and overtopping the swarming multitudes. He was smiling now, throwing a brief word or two to those he knew, but not halting in his determined progress toward the tall girl at the far end of the room.

Jessica looked up and saw him coming. The light from the Green Room lamps gilded his hair, the color of ripe corn and as thick and gleaming as ten-year-old Adrian's. He was tall and broad-shouldered and the eyes that met hers across the space of twelve feet were blue as the sea. His face was still lightly tanned from the sun, and the thought flashed through Jessica's mind that he looked just like a Viking. But the deep voice was surprisingly soft as he murmured an acknowledgement of Lord George's introduction and reached out to take her offered hand in his own large, strong grasp.

"I admired your performance enormously, Miss O'Neill," he was saying.

"Thank you, my lord," she replied, looking straight at him with that beautiful fearless gaze of hers. Gray eyes met blue with a sudden shock of what could have been recognition. Jessica's face was very still.

"I wonder if you would care to drive out with me tomorrow, Miss O'Neill?" said Linton in his grave, soft voice.

There was a brief pause while Jessica continued to look at him. Then she said, "Yes, I should like that very much."

"Damn!" said Mr. Melton to Sir Lawrence Lewis. "If Linton is interested in Miss O'Neill the rest of us may as well retire from the field."

"Unfortunately, you are right, Melton," replied Sir

Lawrence. "What he wants Linton usually gets. And he don't mind paying a high price."

"He's had no one under his protection since the Riviera. And that was at least six months ago."

"Damn!" Sir Lawrence said to Mr. Melton, as he watched Linton smile at Jessica. "I'm very much afraid he *is* interested. I wonder how long he plans to remain in London this time?"

Lord George asked his friend the same thing. "For how long do you mean to remain away from your pigs and your cows, Philip?" he queried Linton humorously as they made their way toward Brooks' later that evening. As Staplehurst was one of the most famous and beautiful estates in the country the references to livestock were seemingly facetious. But Lord George was not as fanciful as it might appear; Philip Romney was in fact one of the most advanced farmers and enlightened landlords in England. He administered all his own estates, and the grinding rural poverty that was affecting so much of England due to the postwar economy and the Corn Laws was not in evidence anywhere on Romney land.

Linton belonged to that diminishing number of wealthy, powerful, landed gentry who were genuinely attached to the land they owned and the people who worked it for them. He was known to every farmer and laborer on his vast estates, and had been since his childhood. The land, to the Earl of Linton, was more than the rents it brought in; it was also the people who cultivated it. Staplehurst, that great golden stone house surrounded by ponds, waterfalls, and Capability Brown's famous park, was also the center of some of the most efficient and profitable agriculture in England.

Linton laughed at Lord George's question. "My sister Maria and her children are planning to remain at Staplehurst through Christmas. Her husband, most unfortunately, is going to Vienna for the Peace Conference and, as Maria is expecting another child in February, she has decided to remain in England." He sighed. "With five children of her own and one more on the way you would think she'd have enough to occupy her mind."

"After you to get married?" said Lord George sympathetically.

Linton's blue eyes looked rueful. "Incessantly. My mother tries to divert her attention, but Maria. . . . Well, suffice it to say that I am in London for a few months at least."

"Until Christmas?" said Lord George with a poker face.

Linton grinned. "Until Christmas," he agreed.

"It is not a very lively time of year for London."

"No." There was a humorous look around Linton's firm mouth. "I shall have to find something to divert myself, won't I?"

Lord George looked at the profile of the man walking beside him. "You already have, Philip."

"Yes, I rather think I may have," replied Linton with enviable tranquility.

# Chapter Five

Have you seen but a bright lily grow
Before rude hands have touched it?
                    —BEN JONSON

Jessica walked slowly around the house in Montpelier Square, looking at everything but in actuality seeing very little. Somehow it didn't seem quite real—the small but elegant house, the matched pair of bays in the stable together with the handsome carriage. Most of all, the money that now reposed in her bank account.

She had gone driving with Philip Rodney and had had supper with him twice. She had found herself liking him very much, much more than any of the other men who had been throwing out lures to her. There was a look of smiling tenderness in his eyes and about his mouth when he looked at her that got immediately under her guard and caused her to relax in his company. The thought crossed her mind that more than one woman had probably been undone by that lazy, sweet smile and those glinting blue eyes.

He had broached the topic that had brought her here with infinite delicacy. He had taken her back to her lodgings after a late after-theatre supper and had sat for a minute beside her in the carriage, his eyes on the narrow, shabby front door of her temporary home. "I have a house in Montpelier Square that is standing empty at the moment," he had said thoughtfully. "It would make me very happy if you would move into it and let me take care of you."

Even in the dim light of the carriage she had been able to see the blue of his eyes. "I cannot afford to run a large establishment," she had answered in a voice that was not quite her own.

"It is not a large establishment," he had returned gently, "and of course I should make you a monthly allowance to enable you to cover all expenses." He then had named a sum that had caused her to blink, and, after a breathless moment she had accepted his offer.

He had sent the carriage to her lodgings this morning and it had brought her and all her belongings to this charming little house. He had bought it, Jessica realized somewhat blankly, solely for the use of his mistresses. There were flowers and a note waiting for her. He would escort her home from the theatre that evening, he wrote. She was to tell the cook to have a supper prepared for them.

For perhaps the first time Jessica realized the enormity of what she had done. She sat down in a delicate chair in her bedroom and stared at the large, silk-hung bed. He was coming this evening. "My God," Jessica said out loud. "I don't have the faintest idea what I'm supposed to *do*." She looked around the room again. "What am I supposed to wear?" she asked the green silk walls. "Or am I supposed to wear anything?" She cast her mind over her collection of nightgowns and, involuntarily, grinned. But it was not a laughing matter and she soon sobered. Jessica was an intensely private person, but she was intelligent enough to realize that at this particular moment she needed advice. With sudden decision she put on her pelisse and went downstairs to order the carriage. She was going to pay a visit to Mrs. Brereton.

Eliza Brereton, one of Covent Garden's staple character actresses, was well equipped to advise Jessica. In her youth she had enjoyed the favors of some of the town's most notable men and she now resided in a comfortable, well-furnished house that was the fruit of her labors. She acted because the theatre was in her blood, not because she needed the money.

Jessica had been frank with her, and Mrs. Brereton had been impressed. "Linton is quite a catch, my dear," she had told Jessica admiringly, and, when the terms of the agreement had been disclosed, her eyes had widened. "He is being extremely generous." She had looked thoughtfully at Jessica. "You are not at all the usual thing, though, my dear. You have Quality."

"I am not the usual thing, Mrs. Brereton," Jessica had replied honestly. "That is why I am here." She met the other woman's gaze directly. "I haven't got the vaguest idea of how I should behave and I hoped you would not be offended if I asked you to advise me."

The old actress looked from the proud, intense face of the girl sitting across from her to the subdued, conservative cut of her merino walking dress. "I see," she said quietly. "Well, you have come to the right person,

Jessica. First, let us have some tea. Then we have some shopping to do."

When Jessica returned to Montpelier Square later that afternoon she had a collection of boxes in the carriage. Much as she had hated spending the money, she realized the necessity. Her own wardrobe was certainly not adequate for her present role. She also had an herbal concoction that Mrs. Brereton had pressed on her. "Take some every morning," the old actress had warned her. "It is not an infallible prevention of pregnancy, but it has a decided efficacy." Jessica had accepted it gratefully. Pregnancy was the one aspect of this whole venture that truly terrified her.

Jessica was performing that evening in a new role, one she had played only twice before, Rosalind in *As You Like It*. Thomas Harris was still adhering to his original plan of offering productions that would be unsuitable to the talents of Edmund Kean, and so far his program had been successful. Jessica's Rosalind had won wide acclaim and Kean, faced with this kind of competition, was preparing yet another part. He would open in *Macbeth* the following night.

Linton had not seen *As You Like It*, yet, and for this performance he had taken a box, which he was sharing with two friends, Lord George Litcham and Mr. Henry Farnsworth. He spoke to them amiably enough at the intermissions, but his attention was clearly centered on the stage, and more particularly on the play's star. Jessica's Rosalind was a joy. She brought to the role all her own qualities of independence, decision, and intelligence. He watched her attentively, enjoying the bell-like tones of her voice and the glint of happiness in her eyes as, dressed in boy's clothes, she teased the unsuspecting Orlando: "There is a man haunts the forest that abuses our young plants with carving 'Rosalind' on their barks; hangs odes upon hawthorns, and elegies on brambles; all, forsooth, deifying the name of Rosalind. If I could meet that fancy-monger, I would give him some good counsel, for he seems to have the quotidian of love upon him."

Orlando, unaware that the disguised boy was in truth his love, protested, and Rosalind shook her head, put her foot up on a fallen log, and replied mockingly. Linton leaned a little more forward in his chair as he watched her. The boy's clothes only served to emphasize the beauty of her flexible young body, the long slim legs, the extraordinary fineness of her narrow waist. The play was delightful, but he found himself impatient for it to end.

Jessica did not share his impatience, but end the play finally did, and shortly she found herself beside Linton in the carriage that was taking them inexorably toward Montpelier Square. He made no attempt to touch her after handing her in and chatted easily during the drive about her performance and the theatre in general. When Jessica confessed to curiosity about Kean's Macbeth he instantly volunteered to take her to see it. They arrived at Montpelier Square more swiftly than she had thought possible and sat down to the champagne supper the servants had ready. Jessica did not usually drink champagne but decided that tonight she might need it, so she allowed him to fill her glass twice. When they had finished he smiled at her, his eyes like sapphires in the candlelight. "I am going to smoke a cigar," he said serenely. "Why don't you wait for me upstairs?"

"All right," she replied as coolly as she could, and rose from the table. A maid was waiting to unhook her dress and brush out her hair. She put on the creamy lace negligée Mrs. Brereton had chosen for her that afternoon, dismissed the maid, and stood waiting. She was nervous, because the whole situation was so strange, but she was not afraid. She knew what the mechanics of sex were; she had not bred horses for nothing. And her instincts told her that this tall, straight, strong, golden-haired man got his pleasure in a perfectly normal fashion. She was not looking forward to the coming encounter, but, she told herself sternly, it was certainly preferable to marriage to Harry Belton.

The door opened and Linton came in. He stood for a moment looking at her, then said quietly, "You are very beautiful, Jessica."

Quite suddenly she smiled. "So are you, my lord," she answered truthfully.

A flicker of surprise showed in his eyes and then he smiled back. He came across to her and lightly touched her hair, unbound and loose on her shoulders. "It is the color of the autumn leaves at Staplehurst," he said, and bent to kiss her.

For a moment Jessica was quite still; then she raised her arms to put them around his neck. His hands were strong behind her back and she closed her eyes. They opened again almost immediately as he lifted his head, moved his hands to her shoulders, and held her away from him. She looked up and found his blue gaze full upon her, narrowed now and puzzled. "This is the first time for you, isn't it?" he asked with dawning astonishment.

Jessica hesitated. "Would it make a difference?" she asked cautiously.

"Certainly it would."

"But why?"

He made a small gesture. "I am not accustomed to seducing virgins."

Jessica stared at him, her mind racing. This was a contingency she had not thought of. She opened her mouth to answer him, and he said pleasantly, "I'll find out soon enough if you lie to me, and I won't be pleased."

Jessica looked at him harder a moment. Her expressive mouth compressed a little. "Yes," she said then. "It is the first time."

"My dear girl," he said in exasperated bewilderment. "I had no idea."

"Well, there must be a first time for everyone, my lord," she said reasonably. "I can't see that it makes all that much difference." An idea struck her. "Oh, do you mean I won't be—adequate?"

"No. That was not what I meant."

"Oh." Her gray eyes were steady on his face. "Then what is the difficulty? Are you saying it would be all right if I were experienced but that you don't want to be the one to 'corrupt' me?"

He was frowning now, his golden brows drawn together. "Something like that."

"It sounds an odd sort of morality to me," she said a trifle tartly.

"I suppose it is." He stared at her intently. "What are you doing this for? Do you really understand the consequences of all this?" and he gestured, comprehensively, to the room and to the bed.

She drew herself up to her full height. "Yes," she said uncompromisingly. "I do."

He smiled a little. "I doubt it. How old are you?"

"Twenty-one." She walked away from him to the fire, and he watched her in silence, observing the grace of her arms and neck and head, the straight beauty of her legs, visible through the thin folds of her negligée. She turned to face him and the firelight lit her hair to copper. "I did not make this decision lightly, I assure you of that, my lord. I need quite a large sum of money and this is the only way I can get it." She paused, then said slowly, "If it isn't you it will be someone else." He did not answer. She made a small movement of her hand and said tentatively, "I would rather it was you. I am a quick learner. I will try to please you."

He thought suddenly that it was wretched of him to make her beg him. He *was* making her, and this for him wouldn't do at all. She was very beautiful as she stood there, facing him in all her desire to persuade, to please. She meant it, he thought. If it wasn't him, it *would* be someone else. He saw her brace herself slightly to meet his refusal. He smiled at her, his blue eyes suddenly full of the familiar lazy sunshine she had found so attractive. "You've convinced me," he said in his soft, slow voice, and held out a hand to her.

Color flushed into her cheeks and her mouth relaxed slightly. She crossed the floor and stood before him once again. "You'll have to show me what to do," she said a trifle unsteadily.

"There's no hurry," he replied, and gathered her lightly into his arms and kissed her again. It was a kiss that was thorough, leisurely, and surprisingly effective. When he finally raised his head she stood for a moment in the circle of his arms, blinking up at him. "Good heavens," she said faintly.

"Good heavens, indeed," he returned in a voice that was huskier than usual. Without further comment he picked her up and carried her over to the bed.

When he departed a few hours later he left a stunned Jessica behind him. She had had no idea her body could react the way it had. After he had dressed and was ready to go he had bent and kissed her lightly on the temple. "It will be better next time," he had promised. The thing that frightened her most was that she believed him.

# Chapter Six

Come live with me and be my love,
And we will all the pleasures prove.
—CHRISTOPHER MARLOWE

If Jessica was unsettled by what had occurred that surprising night Linton was scarcely less so. He had known as soon as he had seen Jessica that he wanted her. Her cool assurance had misled him; he had never dreamed but that she was experienced in the ways of love. He should have remembered that she was an actress, he thought. But she could not disguise her inexperience when he had kissed her. Philip Romney knew women and he recognized the innocence of that tentative kiss. He recognized too that it had only made her more desirable to him. It shouldn't have. He had spoken the truth when he said that virgins did not interest him. But Jessica did, and more than ever after what had happened between them last evening. It had been intense and tender, sweet and lingering. He had been very gentle, aware of her innocence and careful not to offend it. It had been, he thought with a wry smile as he sat over a solitary breakfast the next morning, rather like a wedding night.

He went to considerable trouble to make arrangements to take her to *Macbeth* for Kean's opening performance. The boxes had been sold out for over a week but he managed to procure one from Mr. Martin Wellingford at Brooks' in the afternoon. Mr. Wellingford, a rather nondescript young man who was anxious to make his way in society, was very pleased to do a favor for the Earl of Linton. Linton made a mental note to include the young man in some upcoming scheme of his own, thanked him warmly, and sent off a note to Montpelier Square, telling Jessica he would call for her that evening in order to take her to Drury Lane.

The theatre was packed when Jessica and Linton arrived. There was an electric feeling about the crowd, as if it knew it was present at a momentous occasion. Jessica's appearance in the box with Linton helped to raise the excitement to fever pitch. There was scarcely a person present who had not seen her Juliet and all were well aware that the resounding hit she had made in that part was one of the stimuli for Kean's tackling Macbeth at this particular moment.

"How does it feel to be on the other side of the curtain?" Linton asked, his mouth close to her ear.

She smiled faintly. "A lot less nerve-wracking. But I have seen Kean before. In fact it was he who gave me the idea of acting."

"Really?" He sounded interested. "Where did you see him? He only made his mark in London last spring."

Too late Jessica realized her mistake. She continued

to look at the stage and shrugged a little. "Oh, I scarcely remember; it was a while ago."

He didn't pursue the subject, but his eyes rested speculatively upon her averted head, so beautifully and proudly set on its long neck. She had acted in Ireland, or so the Covent Garden management had given out. Linton didn't think Kean had played in Ireland before the previous summer. Jessica was aware of his scrutiny and felt herself beginning to tense up. She was grateful when the lights began to dim.

The crowd sat in breathless silence through the opening scenes, but when Edmund Kean made his entrance the pit rose and cheered and the women in the boxes waved their handkerchiefs. It was some moments before his harsh voice could be heard above the thunder of appreciation.

At the intermission Linton turned to Jessica. "He dominates the play," he said to her.

There was a faintly ironic look in her eyes. "He certainly does. Lady Macbeth is cast quite into the shade."

He grinned. "I believe you'd like to do Lady Macbeth yourself!"

The corners of her mouth curled. "I?" she said demurely. Before he could answer the door to their box opened and Lord George Litcham and Mr. John Mowbray entered.

"Philip, you dog, do you know what an uproar you have caused by bringing Miss O'Neill? The whole house is agog at the spectacle of two great actors confronting each other across the curtain, as it were."

Lord George turned to Jessica. "How do you do, Miss O'Neill, and how do you like Kean this evening?"

Jessica hesitated, her eyes going to Linton. He met her gaze and realized she was looking to him for guidance. He cut in and said easily, "Miss O'Neill was telling me how much she admired Mr. Kean's performance before you burst in so enthusiastically, George. And that, I should say, was the general consensus of opinion in the house. He is very powerful."

"Yes, he is," said Jessica composedly. "Are you enjoying the play, Mr. Mowbray?"

"Very much, Miss O'Neill," responded that gentleman courteously, but before he could continue the conversation the door opened to admit two more gentlemen. Both Jessica and Linton were quietly friendly, but all the visitors were aware of a distance that surprised them a trifle.

Linton's purpose was to protect Jessica from the overfamiliarity that her now public relationship with him would invite. She herself did not know how to behave. She would see what he would do—so their briefly locking eyes had told him—and she would act accordingly. And he had been swift to set a tone of impeccable courtesy and respect. After a slightly stilted beginning Jessica's own breeding asserted itself. She had been born and reared a lady; she simply behaved in the way that was natural to her. After his friends had departed Linton looked at her with approval. She was dressed in a new gown of wine-dark Italian crape that set off her brilliant coloring. Its neckline was more deeply cut than any she had worn before, but many great ladies in the audience wore gowns even more revealing. She had her mother's diamonds in her ears, but her throat was bare. He smiled at her faintly, his lids half hiding his very blue eyes. It was a smile whose intimacy rather took her breath away. She didn't know whether to be glad or sorry when the curtain rose for the next act.

They went to the Piazza for supper after the play. When they were seated in one of the charming booths and were each sipping a glass of wine Jessica said curiously, "Tell me what you do at Staplehurst, my lord. I gather from Lord George that you spend most of the year in the country."

"What do I do to amuse myself?" he asked smilingly.

She looked a little startled. That was not what she had meant. Jessica, who had worked very hard at Winchcombe all her life, was not a person who thought very much about amusement. "I suppose so," she replied a little uncertainly.

His eyes narrowed a little as he watched her face, then he said truthfully, "I farm."

She looked interested. "Do you? Do you have an experimental farm like Lord Cochrane?"

He put down his glass of wine and regarded her thoughtfully. He had not expected her to know the name of Lord Cochrane. "No, although I find Lord Cochrane's work extremely interesting. My work is more administrative, I'm afraid."

"Do you own a great deal of land?"

"I do. And I am happy to say that the people who work for me now are the people who have farmed Staplehurst land for hundreds of years. Not one family has been forced off my land."

She was surprised by the note of suppressed passion in his voice. "What do you mean?"

He sighed. "I mean that a great change is coming in this country, Jessica. It has already begun, in fact. Today most Englishmen still work on the land or in trades connected to agriculture. That will not be true twenty years from now. Country populations are already moving into the cities to work in industrial factories. The whole face of agriculture is changing. It has become more efficient, more scientific, more centralized. That can be very beneficial, but it also has its drawbacks."

"Drawbacks? How can greater efficiency be a drawback?"

"Because the small independent farmer is no longer efficient. He can't compete. In many cases his farm has been bought by a larger, wealthier landowner. Many of the old smallholders have become landless agricultural laborers. The commons have been enclosed and so cottagers have nowhere to graze a cow or find fuel. We are in a state of transition from an agricultural to an industrial economy and at Staplehurst I am fighting what could be called a holding action."

She was listening to him intently. "At least you are employing a large number of people."

"I am," he replied a trifle grimly, "but unless something is done politically to stabilize the economy the efforts of a few well-intentioned landowners like myself will go for naught."

"Most of the big landlords seem to be pressing for another Corn Law," she said neutrally.

His eyes began to get very blue. "What we do *not* need is to hinder the import of cheap foreign corn. There will be famine if we do it. With 250,000 demobilized soldiers and sailors thrown on the labor market there will be disaster. Wages will be down for those who can get jobs. For those who cannot the Poor Relief will be the only answer. And neither those with jobs at below-subsistence wages or those on Poor Relief will be able to afford corn if it is stabilized at 80 shillings a quarter."

"I have never been much in favor of the Poor Relief," Jessica remarked. "Not, at least, when it is used to supplement wages. It may assist the worker temporarily, but in the long run it benefits the employer, who is relieved of the necessity of paying a living wage. And the small parish taxpayer is forced to subsidize, via the poor rate, the payroll of the big farmer and manufacturer."

"Good for you, Jess," he said strongly. "When I think of the number of people I have tried to impress that fact upon I could weep."

The faint bitterness was back in his voice, and Jessica's eyes fixed themselves thoughtfully upon his face. Under Linton's serene, gentle exterior there evidently lurked the soul of a reformer. "You surprise me," she said frankly.

"Not half as much as you surprise me," he returned. "You are really interested in all this aren't you?"

"Yes." She looked very serious. "I can imagine how

it would feel to be thrown upon the world with nothing behind you, no land, no job, no government to help you out." At the bleak look that touched her face he felt a sudden stab of fierce protectiveness.

"You can always come to me," he said.

"Thank you, my lord," she replied with an effort at lightness. "I shall remember that."

# Chapter Seven

So every sweet with sour is tempered still,
That maketh it be coveted the more;
For easy things, that may be got at will,
Most sorts of men do set but little store.
—Edmund Spencer

Jessica and Linton had not been unobserved at the Piazza. Lord George Litcham and Mr. John Mowbray were seated at no very great distance, and they had been joined by Bertram Romney, one of Linton's cousins. "I wonder what Philip is being so serious about," Lord George commented as he watched his friend with speculative eyes.

"It don't look like a jolly little coze, does it?" replied Mr. Mowbray. As they watched, Jessica said something and Linton replied, the set of his mouth very determined.

"I know that look of Philip's," Mr. Romney said. "I believe he must be talking about the economy."

"To *Miss O'Neill?*" Mr. Mowbray sounded incredulous.

"She doesn't look bored," returned Lord George. All three men looked surreptitiously at Jessica's absorbed face.

"No, she doesn't," agreed Mr. Mowbray.

Jessica and Linton rose to leave, and on their way out passed by Lord George's table. Linton nodded at them in a friendly if abstracted way as he followed behind Jessica. He didn't pause to chat, but took Jessica's elbow in a firm grasp and steered her past the remaining booths and out the door.

"He was in rather a hurry to leave," said Mr. Romney.

"You would be too if you were going home with Jessica O'Neill," said Lord George. And, upon an instant's reflection, Mr. Romney agreed.

Jessica was performing the following two evenings, and the evening after that Linton took her to a very exclusive gaming club in St. James's Square. "My cousin Bertram is very enthusiastic about it," Linton told Jessica. "To own the truth I'd like to see the lay of the land. Bertram is only twenty-four and not very shrewd. The place may be perfectly honest; in fact Crosly and Abermarch assure me the play is fair, but I'll feel better if I take a look myself. Do you care to accompany me?"

Jessica's large gray eyes looked luminous. "To a gaming hell. I should love to go."

He smiled a little. "I shouldn't exactly call it a hell. And why do you want to go?"

"I'd love to see the place where all that money changes hands; where fortunes are lost and men blow their brains out."

He laughed at her. "No one blows their brains out

in the club, Jess. Very bad ton to do that. One waits until one is decently home."

"Too bad," she said cryptically.

"Too bad?"

"Yes. I should love to see some stupid ass who had bankrupted himself and his family blow his brains out right in front of me." The memory of Sir Thomas was still raw in her memory and he winced a little at the note of contempt in her voice.

"Not everyone who gambles bankrupts himself."

"I suppose not. Do *you* gamble, my lord?"

"I have been known to upon occasion," he answered with sonorous gravity.

The corners of her mouth quirked with amusement. "I bet you win, too, you wretch."

"Upon occasion," he repeated serenely, and Jessica laughed.

Mr. Romney had been startled when his cousin had informed him he was bringing Jessica. "But why, Philip?" he had said. "We're going with Litcham and Harry Crosley. She'll be the only woman."

"I have no intention of staying until the small hours, Bertram, and we will meet you there," Linton replied imperturbably. "I am taking Miss O'Neill because she hopes to see someone blow his brains out."

"I beg your pardon?" said Mr. Romney, unsure if he had heard correctly.

"No need to do that," Linton assured him kindly. "We'll see you this evening, Bertram." He began to move away.

"But aren't you dining with us?" Mr. Romney called after him.

"No," came the definite reply.

Bertram was right to be puzzled, Linton thought as he walked down the front steps of Brooks'. Whenever he had joined a party like this in the past they had always commenced with a comfortable dinner and gone on to their destination, a good-humored, high-spirited, all-male group. He was breaking with tradition by taking Jessica. Why?

It was quite simple, really, he thought as he took the reins of his phaeton. He preferred her company to a party of his friends. There was nothing so odd in that, he told himself. After all, she was a very beautiful woman. The fact that no beautiful woman had ever come between him and his bachelor pursuits before was a thought he did not pursue.

Jessica wore the last of her newly purchased gowns, a creamy silk that made her skin seem to glow with a shell-like luster. Linton looked at her bare neck for a moment in silence then said, "Have you no jewelry, Jess?"

The beautiful color in her cheeks deepened. "Very little," she answered shortly. It had all been sold to help pay her stepfather's debts.

"I shall have to remedy that," he said smilingly.

"No!" He looked at her, his blue eyes wide with surprise. "You are very kind," she said with an effort, "but I assure you I do not wish for any jewelry."

"I see," he said equably. He did not see, of course, but there were many things he did not understand about Jessica. After the first few times, however, he had ceased to question her about the things that puzzled him. When she was questioned she became taut and wary and aloof. Philip Romney was one of those large, strong, powerful men who are extraordinarily gentle in all their dealings with those who are smaller and weaker. Jessica was a very independent person who obviously was used to standing alone and asking no quarter of anyone, but he sensed the vulnerability that lurked behind that efficient exterior. He did not want to distress her, so he held his peace and filed away in his formidable memory all of the odd scraps of information she unknowingly let drop.

The gaming house was large and elegant and busy. They were welcomed by Mrs. Farrington, the owner and hostess, who gushed with enthusiasm to see the very rich Lord Linton enter her portals. Lord George, Mr. Romney, and Sir Harry Crosley had already arrived and were playing cards in the blue salon, so Mrs. Farrington informed them. Jessica and Linton then proceeded up the stairs to join them.

It didn't take Jessica long to decide that gambling was an exceedingly tedious pastime. Everyone sat staring, mummylike, at their cards, and even the sight of so much money on the table soon lost its novelty. "Mrs. Farrington said there was a roulette wheel here," she murmured into Linton's ear at last. "I am going to watch that for a while."

"Would you like to wager something for me?" he

asked. She had refused to take any money from him before they came.

She shook her head. "No. I'll just observe." He watched her until she had left the room, then turned back to the table, a slight frown between his brows.

Jessica found the roulette more interesting. At least she could see what was going on. She also met and chatted to several men she knew from the Green Room gatherings at Covent Garden. She had moved away from the roulette game and was standing at the far side of the room looking at a landscape that reminded her a trifle of Winchcombe when she heard a smooth voice say, "I hate to intrude on beauty admiring beauty, but I am really most anxious to meet you, Miss O'Neill." Startled, Jessica looked around to find herself standing next to a tall man of some thirty-five years. He was dramatically good-looking, with coal black hair and strange hazel eyes. "I'm Alden, you know, and I have been longing to tell you how very much I admire you."

Maximilian Chatham, Lord Alden, was a well-known figure in Regency society. He was very rich, very bored, very aristocratic, and very ruthless. He had a bad reputation when it came to women. Jessica had not met him because he had only just returned to London after a stay of several months in France. She looked at him now and did not like him. He reminded her of a horse her stepfather had once owned: very good-looking, but vicious. "Thank you," she said firmly, and turned to move away. He put a hand on her arm.

"Don't run away so quickly," he said softly. "Linton is safely occupied in the card room. Stay and talk to me a little."

She stared silently at his hand and he removed it. "I do not speak to gentlemen to whom I have not been introduced," she said coldly.

A distinctly unpleasant smile curled his thin lips. "But I just introduced myself," he said silkily.

There was a quiet murmur by the door and Jessica turned to see Linton entering the room. He looked around, saw her, and strode purposefully across the polished floor. Jessica's eyes were fixed on him. His hair gleamed like a golden helmet under the bright chandelier, and she met his eyes with a little shock of concussion. "Philip," she said. No one, he thought, had ever made his name sound quite like that. His blue eyes smiled at her.

"There you are, Jess. I've come to take you down to supper." She placed her hand on his arm, and finally he turned to the other man standing next to her. "I didn't know you were back in town, Alden."

"I arrived only a few days ago, Linton, and have been trying to repair some of the ravages of my absence by making Miss O'Neill's acquaintance. She has rather an odd scruple, however, about the propriety of my doing so. Would you be so kind as to present me yourself?"

Linton's blue eyes regarded him inscrutably for a moment. "But if I did that she might feel free to speak to you," he finally said pleasantly. "Good evening, Alden." And turning, with Jessica on his arm, he walked away.

"I don't like him," she said frankly as they went down the stairs. "Who is he?"

"A Bad Man," he replied gravely. "Stay away from him."

"With pleasure," she replied decidedly.

Mr. Romney joined them for supper. Linton sat back and watched with a mixture of amusement and respect as Jessica handled his young cousin. She got Bertram to admit, somewhat to his own surprise, that there were better things to be doing with his life and fortune than gambling. She asked him if he liked horses and listened with grave attention that clearly flattered him as he discussed his favorite pastime at great length. Mr. Romney, whose father had left him a tidy inheritance, had ambitions to race his own horses. Linton thought he could almost see Jessica's attention click as Bertram said that. "I should imagine there are few thrills more exciting than seeing one's own horse cross the finish line first," she said.

Mr. Romney agreed enthusiastically. In fact, he confided, there was going to be a private sale at Sevenoaks on Thursday and he rather thought he might pick up some bargains.

"Hunter selling out?" asked Linton.

"Yes. The whole stable is going," replied his cousin.

"Hunter?" Jessica looked startled. "He's one of the biggest breeders in the country. What happened?"

Two pairs of eyes widened in surprise. "I wouldn't expect you to know Hunter, Miss O'Neill," Romney said naïvely.

"I'm part Irish," Jessica replied glibly. "Of course I know horses. What happened to Hunter?"

Linton folded his hands piously. "The evils of gaming are boundless as the sea. Alas, poor Hunter is the latest victim."

"You're joking me," she said incredulously. "He bankrupted himself gambling?"

"He did."

Jessica's eyes sparkled. "Well, let that be a warning to you, Mr. Romney. I hope in a few years I won't be going to buy *your* horses at a bargain."

"By Jove, I hope not too!" replied Bertram.

"Ah—are you going to the sale of Hunter's horses?" Linton inquired of Jessica.

"Shouldn't think you'd like it," Mr. Romney said frankly. "You do an awful lot of standing about, you know."

"I don't mind standing and I love looking at horses. But you needn't worry about me. I have the bays. I am perfectly capable of going by myself."

"If you want to go I will take you," Linton said firmly. "I had quite forgotten about the Sevenoaks sale. I'd like to go myself."

As they were leaving the club he said to her, "I must thank you for your well-judged words to Bertram. He doesn't really care for gambling that much; he just thinks it is the thing to do. You handled him very well."

She smiled. "He is a nice boy and I've had a lot of practice dealing with boys. In some ways he doesn't seem very much older than my brothers."

"Oh?" He kept his voice carefully neutral. "How old are your brothers?"

"Ten and twelve," Jessica said, her voice suddenly clipped.

Tactfully, he changed the subject.

# Chapter Eight

Desire, desire! I have too dearly bought,
With price of mangled mind, thy worthless ware.
—SIR PHILIP SIDNEY

Jessica was furious with herself for telling Linton
about her brothers. The problem was that this was not
the first such slip she had made. There was something
about this man that disarmed her, lulled her into a
state of comfortable security where she revealed things
she had had no intention of revealing. It just seemed so
natural to be with him, to share thoughts and ideas
with him, that she inevitably slipped and said things
that were at variance with her new identity.

She had to guard against him, and in more ways
than one. It frightened her, the depths of passion he
could provoke in her. She was afraid of what he made
her feel. She found herself thinking about him when
he wasn't present and when he was with her he absorbed her. She felt herself turning toward him as a
flower turns and opens to the warmth of the sun. And
she resisted.

She had been relieved to see him coming toward
her in the roulette room. She had known he would
stand between her and the unpleasant, persistent Lord
Alden. And that was another danger. She mustn't get

into the habit of looking to him for protection. All her life she had stood alone. She mustn't lose her toughness now. Linton was handsome, and charming and considerate, but their relationship was only temporary. By March she would have enough money to pay off Mr. King. Winchcombe would be clear and she could go home to her old life. She would be glad, she told herself sternly, when March finally arrived.

She revealed more about herself at the Sevenoaks sale. When Linton called for her he was pleasantly surprised to find her dressed in boots and a warm gray pelisse that was distinctly unfashionable but admirably suited to a horse sale. She asked him about his own stables, something they had never discussed before, and he admitted that he occasionally raced his horses. "I wouldn't mind picking up a likely mare," he said. "We must keep our eyes out for one."

There was quite a large crowd of people present, walking about the stables and examining the horses. It occurred to Jessica as she walked among them that it was going to prove difficult to resume her own identity and take her place in the horse world as a breeder when her face had become one of the most famous in London. Everyone there seemed to know who she was. Resolutely she beat down the thought, telling herself that people were quick to forget.

They met Mr. Romney, who was there with Sir Francis Rustington, a young man as enthusiastic and rich as he was, and the four of them went round the stables together. By the time they finished, Jessica's status had risen from inconvenient female to resident expert. She didn't say much, but what she did say was informative and to the point. After he watched her feel the legs and look into the mouth of a chestnut colt with professional competence, Mr. Romney burst out, "Where did you learn about horses, Miss O'Neill? You don't miss anything."

She looked at him kindly. "Why don't you call me Jessica? I told you I was part Irish. I grew up with horses. Don't buy this one, Mr. Romney."

"Bertram," he put in.

"Bertram," she nodded gravely. "He looks all right, but his breeding is questionable. There's speed there all right, but neither his sire nor his dam had any staying power at all. Much better to go with the dark bay."

"The Tabard colt?" said Linton.

"Yes. If you can get him for a hundred guineas you've got a bargain."

They moved toward the stableyard where the auction was going to take place and Linton asked "Did you see a mare for me?"

She flashed him a look. He had been very quiet on the stable rounds. The two younger men had not noticed, being full of comment themselves, but Jessica had. "The same one you saw, I should imagine," she returned composedly.

The faintest and briefest glimpse of a smile showed in his eyes. "The Dolphin filly?"

"The Dolphin filly."

The filly they were speaking of was a big, deep-chested chestnut. Neither of them had mentioned her when they had observed her in the stall, and she had

62

not attracted the attention of either Bertram Romney or his friend. Jessica said now, "Her dam was Classic Princess."

Linton nodded, his face never changing. "Well, let us see how many others have their eyes on her." The first horse was brought out and the auction was begun.

Jessica had never seen so many beautiful thoroughbreds for sale. There were mostly yearlings and two- and three-year-olds; the stallions and the best of the brood mares had already been sold privately. Bertram got the bay colt Jessica had recommended and another gray that they all agreed looked likely. Sir Francis was restrained from purchasing a flashy looking black yearling when Jessica said quietly, "Look at his legs." They all watched intently as the groom ran before the horse, trotting it around the ring.

"I don't see anything," Sir Francis frowned.

"Watch him as he comes toward you," Jessica said, her eyes still on the colt. "He throws his feet out sideways."

"So he does," said Linton slowly.

"Well, what about it?" asked Sir Francis.

"He'll never be fast," Linton explained kindly. "I shouldn't bid if I were you, Rustington." So Sir Francis had stood quietly and watched another man get the colt for thirty guineas.

"Thirty guineas!" he complained. "I missed a bargain."

"Not with that foot action you didn't," Jessica said positively. "There are two Moorrunner colts coming up that will prove to be much better buys in the long run. I should bid on one of them if I were you." Sir Francis took her advice.

The sale proved to be extremely satisfactory to all parties. The two young men were delighted with their acquisitions, Linton had gotten the filly he wanted at a surprisingly good price, and Jessica had gotten some experience in what was going to be her future trade. As they were all cold and hungry by the end of the afternoon they repaired to the Sevenoaks Inn for supper. By this time Bertram and Sir Francis regarded Jessica as quite one of their oldest friends, and the party that gathered around the fireside table was merry and comfortable.

"I didn't even know you were interested in that filly," Bertram said to Linton reproachfully. "You never said a word and then you jumped in at the end of the bidding with a fifty-guinea raise in price. You surprised everybody."

"I didn't surprise Jess," Linton said, his eyes going to her face. She looked very beautiful to him as she sat in front of the fire in her russet wool dress. The leaping flames brought out the copper in her hair, braided so neatly into a coronet on top of her head. She turned to answer Bertram, and Linton thought that she had the most beautiful movements of any woman he had ever seen.

"Your cousin Philip is an old hand at buying horses, Bertram. He observes scrupulously the first rule of the game: never let anyone know how interested you are, otherwise the price will go up."

"Oh." Bertram looked thoughtful.

"I say, Miss O'Neill," said Sir Francis admiringly, "you are a regular mine of information. If you ever decide to give up the stage you could always take up selling horses." He spoke jokingly and Bertram laughed readily. At this moment the waiter came over with the bottle of wine they had ordered, so neither of them noticed the stricken look that had come over Jessica's face at Sir Francis' words.

Linton noticed, however and, under cover of Bertram's tasting the wine, he asked her quietly, "What has happened to distress you?"

She took refuge behind an expression of mute aloofness. "Nothing," she replied briefly.

His eyes, so deeply and changeably blue, remained fixed on her face for what seemed to her a very long time. Then he said, "Very well," and turned to speak to Bertram.

He tried to get her to talk about her past during the drive home. It was clear to the meannest intelligence that Jessica's knowledge of horses was far more extensive than any ordinary person's, male or female, would be. But all she would repeat was that she had spent some time around horses in her childhood.

He didn't believe her. For one thing he suspected she had never set foot in Ireland. When he had tried to pin down about where "in the west" she had performed she had replied glibly, "Oh, Wexford." He had not said anything, so she did not realize that Miss Burnley's lamentable lapses in geography had caused her to give herself away. Wexford was most certainly not in the west of Ireland, as Linton, who had visited there, had first-hand reason to know.

And the knowledge she had displayed this afternoon could only belong to someone who had worked or owned or bred horses—race horses—seriously. He pressured her a little, gently, but she had closed up against him. He had looked at her as she sat on the seat beside him, bent slightly forward, braced and on edge, and he had wanted to put his arms around her and beg her to trust him. But he had known such an action would only frighten her more—frighten her, perhaps, into running. And that, he realized, was something that frightened *him*. He did not want to lose her. There was something about her that attracted him as no other woman ever had.

When they reached Montpelier Square he set himself to reassure her. On the surface she seemed perfectly composed but the signs of strain were there to his discerning eye: her air of withdrawal and the austerity of the set of her lips revealed clearly the tension she was feeling. He had some brandy brought up to the bedroom, and taking off his coat and loosening his cravat he stretched himself comfortably on the chaise longue. "You must be cold after that drive, Jess," he said in his deep, warm voice. "Let me give you a splash of brandy."

She was standing by the fireplace, her right hand resting on the marble and her left keeping her skirt from the fire while she held out a foot to the warmth. "Only my feet are cold," she replied.

"Then take your boots off," he told her. As she hesitated he put down his glass, went across to the fire, and picked her off her feet as easily as if she were a child. He sat her down, knelt down himself, and pulled the boots in question off her feet. He then handed her a small glass of brandy. "Drink it," he said sternly, fixing on her his very blue, steady, and now somewhat imperious gaze.

Reluctantly she took it; then, as he continued to stare at her, she sipped it cautiously. It brought tears to her eyes but she could feel its warmth coursing through her. She sipped again, more assuredly, and looked up to find his eyes still on her. Her mouth compressed a little and then, irresistibly, she laughed. "How odious in you to always be right," she said.

"Do you think I'm always right?" he asked serenely.

"Well, I am still waiting to catch you out."

He smiled, leaned back on the chaise longue, and held out an arm. "Come and get warm," he invited. She put her glass down and went to sit in the circle of his arm. Humorously and reminiscently he began to tell her about an incident from his boyhood where he had been, regrettably, very wrong indeed. Jessica lay still against him, listening and absorbing warmth from his big body, and slowly he could feel the tension draining out of her. Her head was pillowed comfortably against his shoulder. He felt the relaxed weight of her and she seemed to him very small and fragile and tender as she rested against him. There rose in him, as there had before, an overwhelming desire to protect. Why this self-contained girl who had, he suspected, more courage and toughness than many men he knew, should call forth this feeling from him he did not understand. But there was a quality of gallantry about her that moved him very much. She was in trouble, that much was clear to him. He wished he could help her, aside from the monthly allowance he was making her. But he knew, without asking, that she would not allow him to. He bent his head and gently kissed the top of her head. "You're tired," he said softly. "I'll go."

She stirred a little and rubbed her cheek against his shoulder. "I'm not tired. Don't go unless you want to."

"All right," he replied after a minute, his lips once again against her hair. "In that case I'll stay."

# Chapter Nine

No more, my dear, no more these counsels try;
                              —SIR PHILIP SIDNEY

On December 21 Linton left London to go to Staplehurst for Christmas. It was a tradition for as many Romneys as could physically manage it to gather under the Staplehurst roof at this particular time of year, and the head of the family must naturally be on hand to greet them. Linton, who enjoyed his large and noisy family, usually looked forward to Christmas. This year, he realized with a flicker of dismay, he did not want to leave London. The cause of this strange reluctance was Jessica. She had upset the pattern of his life, and he was beginning to be a trifle alarmed at himself. It would probably be better to get away from her for a time, he decided. A few weeks at Staplehurst would help him put her in perspective.

The initial feeling of homecoming he had as he drove up the winding avenue of Staplehurst seemed to confirm his wisdom. He came out of the woods and there before him, its golden stone brilliant in the December sun, was the house, serene and sumptuous, surrounded by avenues and sheets of water stretching into the far distance. He crossed a graceful bridge and drove down one of the avenues, across another bridge, and into the stableyard. He was detained for twenty minutes by his head groom, who was patently delighted to see him; then he walked back up the avenue to the house, feeling the familiar peacefulness of Staplehurst seeping into him.

Things did not remain peaceful for long. He was greeted in the hall by his butler and three noisy nephews. "Uncle Philip! We thought you were never coming," said Matthew, the eldest, a boy of thirteen. "School let out days ago. Remember you said you would take me shooting the next time I came to visit you?"

"Me too!" clamored Lawrence, the next nephew in size.

"I want to ride a *big* horse," chimed in John, age six.

"One at a time, if you please!" he laughed at them. "And at least let me get my coat off and say hello to your grandmother." He allowed his butler to help him remove his caped driving coat. "Lady Linton is in the morning parlor, my lord," said his retainer with a rare smile. "May I say how please we all are to see you?"

"Thank you, Timms. Run along for a moment, boys. I'll see you later."

They groaned but obediently began to move away. "It's been *boring* without you, Uncle Philip," John said reproachfully as he went up the stairs. "Why did you stay away so long?"

Linton merely smiled at his small nephew and began to walk in the direction of the west wing. His grandfather had built a magnificent sequence of formal reception rooms around two sides of the old house, but when the family was in residence by itself they used the smaller, more intimate rooms of the old west wing. Lady Linton was sitting alone working on a piece of embroidery when her son came into the room. She recognized his step and looked up instantly, her face lighting with the bright look it always wore whenever she saw him. Her heart swelled with pride as she watched him cross the room toward her, his thick hair gleaming in the winter sunlight. "Hello, mother," he said in his familiar, beloved voice, and she held out a hand to him.

"Philip!" Her dark blue eyes smiled up at him as he bent over her. "It is so good to see you. I missed you. We all did."

"Did you, love?" He sat down next to her on the sofa, an identical smile in his lighter eyes. "I'm sorry, but there was really no bearing Maria another moment."

She sighed. "Dear Maria. She has such a—definite—personality."

He grinned. "She is a boss, you mean. I am very fond of Maria and there is no one I would rather depend upon if I needed help, but she has bullied me ever since I was born. Having five children of her own hasn't altered one iota her determination to mother *me*. I don't know why; I've got a more than adequate mother of my own." He picked up Lady Linton's hand and kissed it lightly.

She smiled at him lovingly. "No one has ever successfully bullied you, my son."

"Not now, perhaps," he retorted, "but when I was a

child I suffered unmercifully from her sisterly interest in my affairs."

Lady Linton moved a little restlessly on the sofa, then stood up to go rearrange some flowers on a side table. She was a woman of sixty or so, with beautifully coiffed white hair and a remarkably flexible figure for her age. "I had better warn you," she said finally. "Maria's friend Lady Eastdean and her daughter Caroline have joined us for the Christmas holidays."

"What!"

"Now, Philip," said Lady Linton pacifically. "Lady Caroline is a beautiful girl. All Maria wants is for you to meet her."

"I do not need Maria to find a wife for me," he said quietly and deliberately, but Lady Linton did not like the set of his jaw. She knew the obstinacy that lay hidden under her son's usually gentle speech and manner.

"You do not have to marry the girl, Philip," she said now, a trifle astringently. "But she is a nice child. There is no need to ignore her just because her mother is one of Maria's friends."

"I hope I have more courtesy than to ignore a guest under my roof," he replied a trifle stiffly. Then, with a glitter in his eyes his mother recognized, he continued, "The fact that it *is* my roof doesn't seem to worry Maria. I don't mind *her* visiting—that is, I do mind but I will put up with it. But it is the outside of enough for her to be inviting half of her acquaintance to join her!"

"Two people are scarcely half her acquaintance," his mother pointed out gently. "And she didn't invite them. I did."

At that he frowned. "You did? But why, mother? Christmas is always a family party."

"I like Lady Caroline," his mother replied. "And it *is* time you were getting married, Philip."

As he went upstairs to his bedroom to change for dinner Linton's brow was furrowed. It did not smooth out when he encountered his sister in the hallway. "Oh, there you are, Philip," she said in her clear, imperious voice. "Come into my room. I want to speak to you before dinner."

Without replying he followed her in, and when she turned to look at him his frown was more pronounced. There was little in Lady Maria Selsey's appearance to produce such an unpleasant look. She was an extremely beautiful woman whose statuesque blonde loveliness had not been impaired by the birth of five children or by her present pregnancy. "Has Mama told you about Lady Caroline?" she demanded immediately.

"Yes," he replied. His clipped voice ought to have given her warning but she plunged on.

"She is the loveliest, sweetest thing Philip. I do not think there is a girl to equal her around today, and as a patroness of Almack's I think I may say I get to see them all. She will be going to London this spring but I wanted you to meet her first."

"Maria," he said in a quiet, dangerous voice, "if you ever do this to me again I swear to you I will humiliate you, mother, and myself by leaving immediately. I will be polite to Lady Caroline this time because mother has asked me to be, but never again. Do you understand me?"

"I understand you," she replied sweetly. "Don't be angry, Philip. I'm only doing this for your own good."

"Maria," he said grimly, "you have told me that ever since I can remember. *Don't help me any more.* What do I have to do to make you understand? I simply cannot keep fleeing from my home."

"Is that why you went to London?" she asked curiously. "Because I mentioned your obligation to get married once or twice?"

"Once or twice?" he almost shouted. "You have nagged me mercilessly for the last three years! There isn't a girl who has crossed the threshold of Almack's that you haven't ruthlessly thrust upon me at one time or another. If you keep it up I won't ever marry, just to spite you."

"You're spoiled rotten, that's the problem," snapped his loving sister. "You've always been the apple of mother's eye. And becoming Earl of Linton at age seventeen was bad for your character."

"Being born ten years before me was bad for *your* character," he answered between his teeth. "It turned you into a bully."

She stared at his set face for a moment and then her lips began to quiver. "What a terrible thing to say to me," she said in a shaking voice. "I am *not* a bully."

Linton could never bear the sight of a woman or a child in tears. "Stop it, Maria," he said irritably and then, as she began to cry in earnest, he went across the room and put his arm around her. "I am sorry," he said resignedly, patting her shoulder. "You are not a bully and I will be nice to Lady Caroline."

"Th-thank you, Philip," she said, wiping her beautiful green eyes. "And I promise not to nag you. I—I miss Matt, you see, and that makes me crabby."

He looked at his sister's bulky figure and real contrition smote him. "I'm a brute," he said. "Invite as many girls as you want if it will amuse you."

"It won't amuse me if you're not around to see them," she sniffed.

He sighed. "Ria, I have every intention of getting married. I know my duty. But give me the freedom to pick my own wife. Please."

Quite suddenly she capitulated. "All right. I promise never to mention the word marriage again—provided you are nice to Lady Caroline."

"I have said I would be," he replied patiently.

"Fair enough." She grinned at him mischievously. "I won't have time for you in a year or so anyway. Annabelle will be making her come out and I shall have to be on the watch for a husband for her."

"Heaven help London's bachelors when you descend on them in earnest," he said comically, and escaped from the room as she picked up a pillow and made as if to throw it at him.

# Chapter Ten

Brown is my love, but graceful;
 And each renowned whiteness
Matched with thy lovely brown
 looseth its brightness.
                                    —ANONYMOUS

Linton met Lady Caroline when he came down for dinner. The company was to assemble in the blue drawing room and Linton was the first one down. He was standing in front of a painting by Angelica Kauffmann when a young girl came in alone. She stopped when she saw him and he smiled reassuringly. "You must be Lady Caroline. I'm Linton, you know. Do come over to the fire where it is warmer."

The girl came toward him, a shy smile on her face. "How do you do, my lord. Mama wasn't ready yet so I came down by myself."

"Quite right," he replied. "I detest waiting around myself. My sister tells me you and Lady Eastdean arrived yesterday. I trust you have been made comfortable?"

She flushed a little and replied eagerly, anxious to reassure him that they were very well taken care of. Caroline was indeed a beauty. She reminded him of a winter rose, so fair and delicate with her golden curls and pink and white face. The eyes she raised to his were the same color as his mother's, dark blue, almost violet. At this moment his sister came into the room, followed by his niece Annabelle. "Uncle Philip!" the girl cried delightedly, and ran across to kiss him.

"Are you indeed grown-up enough to join us, Belle?" he said, smiling down at her.

She raised her chin. "I am sixteen—almost."

He looked struck. "So you are. And getting prettier every day, if I may say so."

She sparkled back at him, a younger more radiant version of her mother. "Of course you may say so," she assured him, and they laughed at each other, the family resemblance between them momentarily remarkable.

They had dinner in the family dining room. When the rest of the party—several aunts and uncles and assorted cousins—arrived tomorrow they would be using the great formal dining room in the north wing, but for tonight Lady Linton had put them in the more intimate room she knew her son preferred. Lady Caroline sat on Linton's right and conversed with him with a sweet seriousness that was peculiarly pleasing. By the time dinner was over Linton had decided that his mother was right—she was a very nice child.

He was true to his word and went out of his way to be kind to Lady Caroline. The assembled Romneys might have overpowered an army, he told her humorously, and if she felt herself overwhelmed she had just to say so.

"Oh, no, my lord," she had replied with her sweet smile. "I can't ever remember having such a good time. Your family is such fun. And Lady Maria has always been so kind to me."

He looked at her, his eyes full of blue lit-up laughter. "Maria enjoys helping people," he said, the gravity of his voice in vivid contrast to his eyes.

"I think she does," replied Lady Caroline. "She might rather overwhelm one at first, but I can never forget what a good friend she was to mama and me when my father died."

He looked a little rueful. "That is the problem with my sister," he said frankly. "Just when you are ready to murder her for her overbearing ways she turns around and does something so damn *good* that you're left with nothing to say."

She twinkled up at him. "I like her. And I like Annabelle and the boys."

"Yes. Well I have to admit I like them too. Do you and Annabelle care to ride with me to the Harley farm tomorrow?"

"I should love to," answered Lady Caroline delightedly.

Maria was true to her word as well and made no attempt to hector her brother, although she watched him shrewdly. She had been very pleased with herself for thinking of Caroline Shere for Linton. The girl was totally unspoiled, beautiful with a touch of gentle seriousness about her that Maria thought would appeal to her brother very much. At first she watched with satisfaction as he went out of his way to be a gracious host to the young girl, but as the week went by a cloud began to darken her magnificent green eyes whenever they lighted on her brother's disgracefully good-looking face.

"I don't understand Philip," she complained to her mother. "He can't hope to find another girl as sweet and as beautiful as Caroline, yet he is letting her slip through his fingers."

"I thought he was being very attentive to the child, Maria," responded Lady Linton. The two women were in Lady Linton's private sitting room where Maria had run her mother to earth in order to air her grievances.

"Oh, he is being charming!" Maria replied bitterly. "He treats her as if she were Annabelle's age—and his niece to boot. Really, mother, I could shake him."

Lady Linton put down her embroidery. "Leave Philip alone, Maria," she said, and there was a ring of authority in her voice. "He will marry when he is ready to."

"And when will that be?"

"When he has fallen in love, I expect," came the firm answer.

Maria's eyes fell. "They have been after him for years, all the mamas with their pretty little daughters. He could marry anyone—and it is not only the earldom. He is just so damn handsome, and *nice*, that girls fall in love with him constantly. But he has never shown any serious interest in anyone."

"He has not found the right girl," replied Lady Linton.

Maria sighed. "I suppose you're right, mother. You needn't worry about me nagging him, at any rate. From now on I plan to leave him strictly alone. If he doesn't like Caroline Shere he will have to find another paragon by himself."

Lady Linton raised her eyebrows. "Do you mean that, Maria?"

"I do." Lady Maria's eyes flickered a little before her mother's shrewd look. "I know how far I can go with Philip, mother," she said in a low voice.

"And you have reached your limit?"

"Yes." A rueful smile flitted across Maria's face. "He almost lost his temper with me. I had to resort to tears. The last time Philip lost his temper with me he was nine years old and I was nineteen. It was an occasion I still remember vividly."

"So do I," her mother said drily.

Maria smiled at her tone. "Philip's tempers are much less frequent and much less noisy than mine. However, they are far more unnerving. When he starts talking through his teeth I know it is time to capitulate."

"He is so like your father," Lady Linton said softly.

"Well, perhaps there's hope yet," Maria answered with an attempt at humor. "After all, Papa got married."

"Philip will get married too. It is just a question of his finding the right girl."

"I suppose so. But I am beginning to wonder what kind of girl *will* make an impression on such a hardened case."

"That must be for Philip to decide," said Lady Linton. Then, with a pensive look in her eyes, she admitted, "Shall I tell you the truth, my dear? I had hopes of Lady Caroline too."

Linton was asking himself many of the same questions his mother and sister were posing about him. He even tried to drum up a little enthusiasm for the sweet tempting morsel that was Caroline Shere, but he failed dismally. She was a lovely, charming, delightful child but she did not interest him. He found himself spending more time than was comfortable thinking of a reserved and sensitive face with crystal gray eyes set off by extraordinary black lashes and brows. He worried about her. In the middle of the joyous festivities of Christmas Day his thoughts went winging back to London. Was she lonely? Did she miss him? The longer he was away from her the clearer it became that he was missing her.

He held out for two more weeks after Christmas. He was to drive his two eldest nephews back to Eton, and he told his mother he would not be returning to Staplehurst.

"But why, Philip?" she had asked, a faint line between her delicate brows. "Maria has been very good lately. And she is leaving for Selsey Place in a few days anyway."

"It isn't Maria, mother," he replied. "And I think she should stay here, by the way. I don't like the idea of her by herself at Selsey. Why doesn't she wait until after the baby is born?"

"I agree with you but there is no moving Maria. All her children were born at Selsey, she says, and this one will be too."

"As if Matt cared."

"Maria does, unfortunately. I shall go to Selsey myself in a few weeks' time. Certainly she can't be left alone with just the children and the servants."

He frowned a little. "That will leave nobody here at Staplehurst."

"Not if you are in London," his mother agreed gently.

"Well, I shall probably be back before you leave," he said. "And everything is in order here. Should something come up a message can always be sent to Grosvenor Square. I can be back here in a few hours."

"I am sure we shall manage, Philip," his mother told him, and gave him an unshadowed smile. Something was drawing him back to London, and his refusal to confide in her made her think it was a woman. If that was so it explained somewhat his lack of interest in Lady Caroline Shere. Lady Linton was far too wise to question her son. She determined to get her information elsewhere.

Matthew and Lawrence were pleased to be going back to school. They chattered unceasingly during the whole drive, thrilled that they were being returned in a smart phaeton driven by their magnificent uncle. "I'll bet everyone else is sent in a stuffy coach!" Lawrence said scornfully.

"Yes," agreed Matthew. "I hope Geoff is around so he can see your horses, Uncle Philip."

"Who is Geoff?" Linton asked his eldest nephew.

"Geoffrey Lissett, my best friend. His family raises race horses and Geoff helps to train them. Isn't he lucky? He said I might come and visit them this summer if it is all right with mamma. I asked her this

Christmas and she said I might." He gave a little wiggle of anticipation. "Geoff will love your grays. He is even more horse-mad than I am," he confided.

But the Lissetts had not yet arrived at Eton to Matthew's disappointment, and Linton deposited them, gave them both a guinea, put up in town for the night, and left the next morning for London.

# Chapter Eleven

O make in me these civil wars to cease;
I will good tribute pay, if thou do so.
                    —SIR PHILIP SIDNEY

The weeks of Linton's absence had seemed very long to Jessica. She had written to Miss Burnley and the boys telling them she would not be home for Christmas and giving them an imaginative description of the slow decline of the mythical Cousin Jean. She had written four pages of instructions to Geoffrey telling him what to do about the horses during his weeks at Winchcombe. Geoffrey was only twelve years of age, but he was extremely reliable and competent. Jessica had depended on him heavily all during last summer and he had not failed her.

It was her first Christmas away from Winchcombe, her first Christmas away from her brothers. She knew they would be missing her, and her heart ached when she thought of them but, to her consternation, it was not her brothers whose absence preoccupied her most. It was impossible to deny to herself that she missed Linton. Jessica was not a person who shrank from facing the truth, but she found herself seeking excuses for her inexplicable feelings. He was the only person she really knew in London, she told herself. Of course she felt lonely and displaced when he was gone. If she had been at Winchcombe with her family, Philip Romney would be very far from her thoughts. When she went home in March she would forget him.

Linton arrived in London at midday. He spent some time that afternoon at Rundell and Bridge's, a fashionable jewelers, and then stopped by Brooks'. He found Lord George Litcham there.

"Philip!" His friend looked extremely surprised to see him.

"How are you, George?" Linton replied easily.

"Surprised to see you here," Lord George said frankly. "I thought you'd be at Staplehurst until the start of the season.

"I felt the need for a respite from my family," Linton replied somewhat mendaciously.

Lord George rolled his eyes sympathetically. "Lady Maria still visiting, eh?"

"Yes," replied Linton, ruthlessly sacrificing his sister's reputation. "I am exceedingly fond of Maria, but . . ." He paused eloquently.

"I know," replied Lord George. "Sisters!" He had three of his own and knew whereof he spoke. Linton grinned and Lord George continued, "I suppose that means you won't be giving up Miss O'Neill for a while."

"What do you mean?" snapped Linton, a decided edge to his voice. "Of course I am not giving up Miss O'Neill."

"Well there is no need to chop my head off," Lord George said, giving his friend a puzzled look. "I just thought, since you usually stay at Staplehurst until April . . ."

"Well I am not at Staplehurst now," Linton interrupted, his voice clipped with rising temper. A thought struck him, and he fixed glittering blue eyes on Lord George's pleasant, good-natured face. "What has been going on here while I was away?" His voice sounded distinctly dangerous.

"Nothing! Good God, Philip, stop looking at me like that. Nothing has happened. No one has even seen Miss O'Neill except on the stage." He looked at Linton's face for a moment in silence and then said, "She doesn't come into the Green Room and no one is allowed into her dressing room. I know because there are a number of men who have tried to see her. I was not the only one who assumed you may be bowing out."

Linton drew himself up to his impressive height. "Well, you were all wrong," he said grimly. "Good day, George." And he walked away, leaving an extremely puzzled Lord George staring after him.

Jessica was performing that evening, which was why Linton had stayed away. When he finally saw her he wanted her undivided time and attention. And this evening's performance had a special significance, as he had discovered from Mr. Mowbray whom he had met in Bond Street. On January 2 Edmund Kean, at the strong but misguided insistence of the Drury Lane committee, had appeared as Romeo. It was not at all the sort of role suited to him. It was impossible for him to look like a boy, and the ardor of young love was an emotion he found difficult to project. For the first time he invited direct comparison to Jessica, whose Juliet was considered a masterpiece. She was playing Juliet tonight for the first time since the end of December, and the public, with Kean's performance in mind, had come to test hers against it.

Linton waited until the play had begun before he slipped into his seat. He did not want Jessica to know he was there until he could face her directly. When she came on stage he was almost immobile, his eyes closely following her, knowing by heart her special beauty of movement and line, her springing, intense vitality that reached out and captured every man in the audience as surely as the enraptured Romeo.

When the play was finally over the audience rose, cheering and shouting, giving notice, in case anyone had doubted, that Jessica O'Neill owned *Romeo and Juliet*. They quieted only long enough for Thomas Harris to make an announcement: "Ladies and gentlemen, two weeks from tonight I am happy to tell you that Jessica O'Neill will perform in William Shakespeare's *Macbeth*." As the theatre went wild, Linton thought with a wry smile, so she is carrying the war into *his* territory now.

Jessica had taken her costume and her makeup off and was sitting in front of the dressing table mirror brushing her hair when there came a knock on the door. "I am not seeing anyone, Jenny," she said to the girl who was hanging up her costume, and the girl nodded and went to the door.

When she saw who was there her eyes widened, but

he shook his head gently at her and motioned her out. Obediently she slipped past him and he entered the room, closing the door behind him. He stood for a minute, watching Jessica at the dressing table. Her back was to him and, unaware of his presence, she went on serenely with what she was doing. Her head was tipped a little to one side as she brushed, and her hair fell over her bare shoulders, a shining rippling mass of autumnal silk glinting with threads of copper as she stopped and swung it back from her face. "Who was it, Jenny?" she asked, and turned her head, beautiful as a flower on its stem. Her eyes met his, and he heard the sudden sharp intake of her breath. "Philip!"

"Did you miss me?" he asked, and crossed to the dressing table to raise her up. His hands on her bare shoulders, he looked for a minute into her large gray eyes, his own narrow and brilliant in his intent, concentrated face. Then his mouth came down on hers.

The hardness of his kiss surprised her. It was different from the way he had kissed her before. More demanding. Hungry. She remained passive within his arms at first, still surprised by his sudden appearance. Her head lay back against his shoulder, the mantle of her hair streaming over his arm. She felt his body, strong and hard against hers, and slowly her mouth answered to the urgency of his, her response gathering force and passion, her body arched up against his, her arms holding him closely. After a long time he raised his head. His blue eyes were blazing. "Jess," he said.

She laughed unsteadily. "Where did you come from?" His eyes were on the sofa, and he didn't answer. They could lock the door, he was thinking. But no, that wasn't what he wanted, what he had waited all day for. He wanted time with her. Time to bury himself in the inexhaustible depths of her.

"Let's go home," he said, his voice harsh in his own ears.

"All right." She looked around, then, bewildered. "Where is Jenny? I need my dress."

"I sent her out." He looked once more at her bare arms and throat, luminous against the white of her fine camisole. "I'll get her and wait for you outside."

Her eyes, gray as the dawn, met his. "All right," she said again, very softly this time.

When she joined him in the carriage he didn't speak, and she sat beside him, careful not to touch him. The drive to Montpelier Square seemed interminable, and by the time they arrived they were both nearly frantic. They walked together in the front door and, still not speaking, went directly upstairs to the bedroom. Jessica was quivering all over, conscious only of the man beside her, aching for him to touch her.

Her maid appeared, and he sent her away. He turned Jessica around and, still in silence, began to undo the hooks on her dress. She stepped out of it, leaving it lying on the floor, and with trembling hands sat down to take off her stockings. When she looked up he had his shirt off and she stared in fascinated wonder at his broad chest and shoulders, so astonishingly strong and muscular under that well-cut, elegant coat. "I missed you," she told him huskily, answering

**89**

the question he had asked back in her dressing room an hour ago.

He held out his hands and she came to him, melting against him, her eyes closing. He bent over and his mouth found hers.

It was the first time she had let her barriers down. His unexpected arrival had thrown her off balance, and then the irresistible demands of her body, which had recognized him the first time their eyes had met, had taken control. A curious sense of fatalism settled over her now as she lay beneath him, relaxed and at peace, cherishing the feel of his weight as it pressed her down into the bed. She ran her hand caressingly through his hair and it sprang, sparkling like new-minted gold, from her fingers. His breathing had finally slowed. Whatever happens, she thought, I shall always have the memory of this.

Half an hour later she was closed up against him, watching him with open, remote eyes that filled his soul with bitter anger. He had given her a ruby-and-diamond necklace.

# Chapter Twelve

They love indeed who quake to say they love.
                                    —SIR PHILIP SIDNEY

It was a Christmas present, he told her. He had commissioned it before he left for Staplehurst. "I meant to give it to you earlier this evening," he said as he put it into her hands, "but I forgot."

It was exquisite: delicate and glowing and obviously very expensive. She didn't want it, but she knew, looking from the spill of gems in her hand to his face, that she would have to accept it.

"Thank you," she said in a voice she strove to keep even. "It is very lovely."

There was a long pause as he took in the deadness of her tone. She was sitting up in the center of the bed, her back straight, her hair spilling over her white shoulders, the bedside lamp lighting her thick lashes and clear profile. He stood looking at that shuttered, remote face and felt the bitterness begin to rise in his heart. "You don't want it," he said.

"I did not say that."

"You didn't have to. It is written all over your face." He moved away from her and began to dress. "Well, it is yours," he said after a moment. "Do with it as you like. You can always sell it; it is worth a significant amount of money."

Jessica flinched as if he had struck her across the face, but he didn't seem to notice. A lock of bright hair had fallen over his forehead, and impatiently he pushed it back, away from the ice blue of his eyes.

She couldn't speak. She felt frozen, numbed to the heart by what she saw in his eyes. I have never seen him like this, she thought. "Do you want me to leave?" she asked, and in spite of herself her voice quivered.

He stood looking at her for a minute, and his mouth set like a vice. "No. I believe you said you wished to go to the opera tomorrow evening. I'll call for you then." He nodded to her curtly. "Good night, Jess," he said, and left.

Jessica slept very little and arose the next morning with a heavy head. She tried to study her lines but they seemed to slip from her mind as soon as she said them, and the character of Lady Macbeth eluded her completely. She ate very little and didn't notice the worried way the servants looked at her. They had seen many women come and go in that house on Montpelier Square, and everyone was in agreement that they wanted to see Jessica stay. Peter, the footman, had seen Lord Linton leaving last night and it was clear, he reported to the kitchen contingent the next day, that my lord had been very angry. As no one had ever remembered seeing Linton angry before this report cast a pall over the house which was not alleviated by Jessica's obvious depression.

She took a long time getting dressed that evening. She wore the cream silk dress that was her favorite and noticed, with a detached part of her brain, that her skin looked more luminous than usual and her breasts fuller. The maid picked up the ruby necklace from where it lay on top of the dressing table. "It's beautiful, miss," she breathed, and started to put it on Jessica.

It looked magnificent against the white column of her throat. The maid was fastening the catch when Jessica said in a harsh voice, "Take it off. I am not going to wear it."

"But miss," the maid said, shocked into speech, "didn't Lord Linton give it to you?"

"Yes." Her throat felt tight. Part of her wanted to wear it, wanted to please him and placate him, but the other part of her thought in horror of all the people in the theatre who would stare at it and know it for what it was: a payment. She couldn't bear it. "Take it off," she said again.

She was ready and waiting for him downstairs when he arrived. His gaze flickered over her briefly, noting her bare throat, then he said drily, "If you are ready let's go. I don't like to keep the horses standing."

It was a long and painful evening for Jessica. She loved music but scarcely heard a note of the opera. Every nerve end in her body was conscious of him, sitting so close beside her, keeping himself to himself. Her overtures of peace were met with a perfectly courteous, solid resistance. Jessica was discovering what Linton's family had known for years: he was not easily angered, but when he was he was not easily pacified. She thought, as she stole a glance at him from under her lashes, that she had been right when she had first likened him to a Viking. His subsequent gentleness had seemed to negate the comparison, but looking now at his beautiful, clean profile, his firm, merciless mouth, it did not seem so farfetched. When the lights came up for the intermission he turned to her, and it seemed as if the cold, blue North Sea glittered in his eyes.

She gave up trying to reach him and retreated herself behind the cool, aloof expression that had been her camouflage for so many years. Their box was crowded with Linton's friends during the intermissions, and Jessica responded to all questions and comments with a distant politeness that was like a shield between her and them. At one point she looked absently out over the opera house and her eyes came to rest, inadvertently, on the box opposite to Linton's. There was a single man in it, standing watching her with an expression on his face that made her shiver. Lord Alden bowed to her, a slight smile lifting the corners of his thin mouth. Jessica stared right through him and, instinctively, took a step closer to Linton. Alden saw it and laughed.

They went to the Piazza for supper, and they might have been two strangers with nothing between them but a common experience at the opera. Jessica's face was utterly remote, her voice cool and impersonal as she discussed the opera of which she had heard not a note. He accompanied her back to Montpelier Square but did not come in. "I promised Crosley I would meet him at Watiers," he said easily. "Good night, Jess. Sleep well." He kissed her hand lightly and went back out through the door to the waiting carriage.

She did not see him again for five days. She fought against missing him, fought to maintain her defenses and protections. She sought refuge in her work. The production of *Macbeth* had not been Jessica's idea. Thomas Harris, exultant at Kean's failure as Romeo, had conceived the idea of challenging him with material he had made his own. Not only did Harris have Jessica for Lady Macbeth, but a new actor had appeared on the Covent Garden horizon. Lewis Garreg, a young Welshman, had been recommended to him by an acquaintance who had seen him perform in Shrewsbury, and Harris had given the young man a contract. He was also giving him the part of Macbeth.

Garreg knew that it was the chance of his lifetime, and he was both eager and apprehensive. He was twenty-six years of age, of medium height with dark brown hair and clear hazel eyes. He was broadly built and had a voice like an organ, a deep, rolling baritone. He had been very nervous with Jessica at first, but her friendly, calm, professional demeanor soon began to put him at ease. They spent several hours discussing the play and the characters and came up with an interpretation they both felt comfortable with.

"It will be different from the usual portrayal," Jessica had said, "but it has to be, I think. We are both of us much younger than the actors who usually do *Macbeth*. Not that Kean is old, but somehow he never manages to look very young, does he?"

95

Garreg thought of Kean's Romeo and chuckled. "No."

"Well, I certainly can't play Lady Macbeth as the fiendish devil that Mrs. Siddons made so famous. It wouldn't look right. I shall play her as a young woman who loves her husband and who wants, desperately, to see him king. Her weakness is that she does not understand the consequences of the murder she pushes him to commit."

"You don't think she dominates him, then?" he had asked carefully.

"I think there is a balance to the play, Lewis," she answered. "I do not want to dominate it. Macbeth must be a strong man or her love for him makes no sense—she, certainly, is a strong woman. She is able to influence him due to the fact that he loves her also. I see them as two ambitious, proud people who, tragically, destroy each other."

His hazel eyes had blazed. "Let us get started then."

But rehearsals had proved frustrating. Jessica liked to have all of her movements worked out before she went on stage, and her actions, for this play, depended on another actor as they never had before. It was the relationship between Macbeth and his wife that interested her, and she felt as if she were working in a vacuum. She and Lewis Garreg finally sat down together to decide on their movements, but the carpenters were working in the theatre and it was noisy, so Jessica suggested they go to Montpelier Square where they could work without interruption.

They worked all of Wednesday afternoon and made excellent progress. By Thursday they were ready to rehearse the first three acts. They had not gotten through Act One when, unnoticed, Linton walked in. He watched in silence as a burly young man put his arms around Jessica. "My dearest love," a deep, rich voice intoned. The young man looked down into her face. "Duncan comes here tonight," he said, and Jessica's eyes, looking past him, widened.

"Philip!" she said in astonishment, and the burly young man jumped.

Linton looked steadily back at their two startled faces. "I appear to have come at an inopportune moment."

"Well, you did, rather," Jessica replied candidly. "We were rehearsing. May I present Lewis Garreg, Philip, who is to play *Macbeth* with me next week. Lord Linton, Lewis."

Lewis Garreg was extremely uncomfortable. He knew, of course, about Jessica's relationship with Linton, and he did not at all care for the expression in Linton's very blue eyes. "We have been working on the play, my lord," he hastened to second Jessica. "I hope you do not mind?"

"Did you want me for some reason, my lord?" said Jessica in a deceptively gentle voice. She did not care for Linton's look either, and she felt her temper rising.

"I came to see if you cared to go driving with me." There was an audible note of anger in the usually soft tones of his voice.

Their eyes met and locked, and Lewis Garreg instinctively dropped his own gaze. When he looked up again he saw two people whose faces were calm, assured and devoid of passion, but he had seen the anger in those two pairs of eyes now so veiled and cool, and he closed his book with an audible thump. "I'll be going, Jess," he said to her. "I'll see you at the theatre tomorrow. Good day, my lord." With considerable dignity considering its haste Lewis Garreg made his departure, leaving Jessica and Linton alone together.

# Chapter Thirteen

Love is a great and mighty lord
—GEORGE PEELE

There was silence in the room until they heard the front door close behind him. Then Linton said, "Your *Macbeth* will be a sensation if that was a sample."

"Would you care to explain what you mean by that remark, my lord?" she asked in a brittle voice.

"I mean that you and that actor looked very cozy," he said, a grim look about his mouth.

A deep, familiar coldness came over Jessica as she looked bleakly back at him. Just so had she stood many times before, alone and in bitter opposition to her stepfather. As she stiffened her back against Linton he took two steps closer to her and halted. A shaft of pale sunlight from the window fell on his thick blond hair and illuminated his grim, white face and blue eyes. Her own eyes widened for a moment, arrested, and it suddenly was though the veil that had blurred her vision for so long had ripped away and she was standing, naked and defenseless, before the frightening truth. She took a deep, shuddering breath. Her throat ached. All her anger died away, to be replaced by a despair so absolute that it withered her soul. It was pain to look at him. Her eyes fell. "I'll pack and be gone by morning," she said tonelessly.

He had seen her eyes before the lids came down. "What is it, Jess?" he asked, his voice gentler than it had been. "What is the matter?"

She shook her head hopelessly. She could not tell him. She could not even blame him for thinking of her and Lewis Garreg as he did. "Do you understand the consequences?" he had asked her on their first night together. She had not, she thought now, with pain a hard knot inside her. Never in a million years had she dreamed that she would fall in love with him. She made a small gesture that was like the cry of a lost child. "I'll go," she repeated doggedly.

He came closer. "Where will you go?"

Her mind went blank at the question. Where? Home? But she still did not have the money for the mortgage. To another man? Blindly she shook her head and wrapped her arms protectively around herself. She could not answer him.

He put his hand under her chin and tilted her face up. Her eyes, wide and distraught with unhappiness, met his. The cool composure that had been her shell for so long was destroyed. "Do you love this Garreg fellow?" he asked painfully.

"No!" She stepped back, away from him, away from the temptation to throw herself into his arms, to tell him it was he she loved. It was no good, she thought. Love was not in the bargain they two had made.

Linton was silent, his blue eyes strangely impersonal, looking into her eyes as if he were trying to find the truth that was hidden there. She stared back as if hypnotized by that steady and intent gaze. "Jess," he finally said quietly, "why won't you wear my necklace?"

She tore her eyes from his and turned to walk to the window. She rested her forehead against the cold glass and closed her eyes. "Because it makes me feel like a whore," she said wearily. "Which is a very stupid reason, I know, since that is exactly what I am."

There was a stunned silence, then he said in a voice that was barely audible, "Oh my God." She didn't move and he came across to where she stood at the window. "Do you think that is how I regard you?" There was a note in his voice that pierced the fog of despair that was engulfing her, and she turned slowly to face him.

"How do you regard me?" she asked simply, all defenses shattered.

"I regard you as the woman I love," he answered, and reached out to pull her into his arms. The relief she felt was so intense that her knees buckled. He held her close and she pressed against him. She was shaking.

"Philip," she said. "Philip."

"I gave you that necklace because I love you," he was saying. "I'd spin the moon out of the sky to give you if I thought you wanted it."

"I just want you." Her voice was muffled by his shoulder.

She felt so slim and light in his arms. "I'm sorry, Jess. I'm sorry, darling." His lips were against her temple. Then, suddenly, his hands were hard on her shoulders, holding her away from him. She looked up to meet his eyes. They were bluer than the sea on a summer day, and deeper. "Don't ever say that about yourself again. Do you hear me?"

Mutely she nodded.

He smiled a little, and her own eyes, clear as the sea but not of its color, smiled back. "Do you still want to go driving?" she asked huskily.

"No," he replied, his hand lightly touching her mouth. "I have another idea."

They went upstairs to the bedroom and stayed there until noon the next day.

For Jessica the world had changed. When she had embarked on this enterprise her intentions had been solely monetary. It had never once crossed her mind that she might fall in love. But she had never imagined that a man like Philip Romney existed in the world.

He was a man she could trust. She had known that, instinctively, from the moment they first had met. With everyone else she had ever known she had had to play a role; she had had to be strong and resolute, fearless and independent. For some reason only he had the power to force her outside her defenses. He had caused her to strip away all her protections, layer by layer, until she was left vulnerable and defenseless before him.

And she was happy as she had never been before. She let go her hold on herself, she relinquished herself to him. All her doors at last were open. "I love you," she whispered to him deep in the night. "You own me, body and soul, do you know that?"

His mouth was on her, feeling her silken smoothness as she lay there, open to him as a flower lies open to the sun. His voice, when it came, was husky and unsteady. "The things a man owns, my darling, hold him far more securely than he holds them."

She smiled. "Then we own each other."

He did not answer her in words.

When they woke for the last time the sun was slanting into the room through the drawn blind. She stirred in his arms. Her eyes focused dreamily on the bedpost, and she lay still, listening absorbedly to some inner voice. "I'm hungry," she said finally in a surprised tone. Then, more strongly, "I'm starving. What time is it?"

"I don't know," he said calmly, as if it was not of the slightest importance, and she sighed and rested her head on his shoulder. The minutes ticked by.

"If I don't get some food soon I am going to expire," she said at last in a sepulchral tone, and he chuckled.

"We'll get up." They didn't move. She listened to the beating of his heart, so steady and reassuring. She yawned a little, and he kissed her lightly and sat up. "I'll ring for one of the servants." He went across to the wardrobe and pulled out a green velvet robe which he tossed to her. "You'd better put that on," he advised, sliding his arms into his own dressing gown.

They had breakfast brought up to the bedroom. Jessica ate hugely. It seemed to her she had never been this hungry before. By the time they had finished Linton's valet had arrived from Linton House in Grosvenor Square. Linton had sent for him to bring a change of clothes. He used the dressing room off Jessica's room while she dressed in the bedroom. When he was attired in biscuit pantaloons, well-polished Hessian boots, and a blue coat of Weston's superb tailoring, he went into her room. She was seated in front of the dressing table having her hair done.

"I have to go down to Holland House this afternoon," he told her. "Would you like to go to dinner at Grillon's this evening?"

"I would like that very much," she assured him as her maid put the last pin in her hair. "I'm going to the theatre this afternoon. *Macbeth* opens next week and Mr. Harris is probably having apoplexy about now."

He grinned. "I hope that Garreg fellow hasn't reported that I've murdered you."

"I'm sure Miss Favel is hoping," she replied, referring to her understudy.

"I'll drive you there if you're ready," he offered, and she rose promptly and accompanied him downstairs.

He was driving his grays. The winter day was cold and clear, making driving in the open phaeton a pleasure. She sat close beside him and neither of them spoke. He watched the road through the ears of the horses, driving with steady attention through the busy London streets. Only now and then did she turn to look at him, at his profile clean as a chiselled thing as he studied the road with grave intent. One of her hands was in her muff, the other, gloved in soft kid, lay relaxed on her lap. Without looking at her he put his own upon it and covered it. She gave a faint smile but said nothing. When they reached Covent Garden she disappeared quickly inside the theatre, and he drove on toward Kensington.

# Chapter Fourteen

What's done is done.
—WILLIAM SHAKESPEARE

Jessica worked as hard as she ever had in her life during the following week. Her own happiness with Linton distracted her and she found herself having a very difficult time getting a grasp on Lady Macbeth. She had built the character, as she always did, from the outside in. She knew what gestures she would make, how she would hold her head, where she would move on the stage and when. But that inner spark of concentration, which enabled her to project the essence of the character through this outward guise she had created, was missing.

She rehearsed with dogged persistence, spending the whole day in the theatre and then the night with Linton. She was looking very beautiful, with a silvery radiance to her face that drew men's eyes like a magnet. She tried to concentrate on *Macbeth* but her thoughts kept slipping away to rest on lazy, laughing blue eyes, strong, long-fingered hands, a mouth full of determination and of humor, that yet could look so tender . . . "You're on, Jess," said Thomas Harris testily, and she pulled herself from her reverie to hear Garreg repeating, "How now? What news?"

With an apologetic glance at Harris she walked on stage and crossed to Lewis Garreg. "He has almost supped," she said clearly. "Why have you left the chamber?" But ten minutes later her mind had wandered again and she missed another cue.

Linton was surprised by the amount of time Jessica put in preparing for the opening. He himself had spent one whole afternoon giving her her cues so that she could get her lines down. "Somehow one doesn't think of actors having to memorize a part," he said to her.

Jessica smiled, white teeth flashing in the grave intentness of her face. "How did you think we learned the lines, then?"

"I didn't think about it at all. One just assumed that you were born knowing them, I suppose."

"It would be much easier if we were," she replied fervently. Then, a minute later, as she missed a line in the murder scene, "Damn! I can't ever remember having such trouble committing a part to memory. And Lady Macbeth has far fewer lines than Juliet or Rosalind." She closed her eyes, frowning. "Let's do it again."

Obediently he flipped back in his script. "Act II?"

"No. Let's start from the beginning."

"You may not know your lines but I certainly am getting to know Garreg's," he replied humorously. "All right, begin with the letter."

She got up and began to pace around the room.

"They met me in the day of success . . ." she began with energetic determination, and he followed along in the script, stopping her when she made a mistake. By the end of the day she had the lines down letter perfect. But still the character escaped her.

The night of the opening Jessica went to the theatre early and by herself. "You'll only distract me," she had told Linton, the glimmer of a smile in her eyes.

"Will I? Good." Then, as she had shot him a look, half amused, half exasperated, he had given in. "All right. I'll stay away. But afterwards we'll go out to supper."

"All right."

"You are really nervous, aren't you, Jess? I've never seen you like this before."

"You've never seen me before I've opened in a new part!" she retorted. "If you think I'm nervous now you should have seen me before I first went on as Juliet. I didn't think I'd be able to speak at all that night, let alone remember the lines."

"Well, considering that it was your first time on stage, it's understandable," he said.

He had caught her entirely off guard. "I suppose so. At any rate I was petrified." Then, as the magnitude of her admission hit her, her head jerked up and she stared at him warily.

His blue eyes glinted through narrowed lids. "I never did believe that story about the west of Ireland," he said gently.

"Oh." She thought for a minute. "Why?"

"Wexford, my darling, is on the east coast."

Quite suddenly she grinned. "My dreadfully inadequate education comes home to roost. No, I was never in Ireland and yes, the first time I ever set foot on a stage was when I played Juliet at Covent Garden."

"Quite a jumping-off point for a beginner," he commented neutrally.

"It wasn't my idea," she replied vigorously. "I was looking for a small part, a lady of the court or something like that. It was Mr. Harris's brilliant notion to cast me as Juliet. I even tried to talk him out of it, but he was determined." She sighed. "I would infinitely prefer to be more anonymous. I had no intention of becoming famous. It is—rather uncomfortable at times. But, as Lady Macbeth so eloquently says, 'What's done is done.' "

He looked at her in silence, taking in the clear burning brightness of her, then he asked quietly the question that had haunted him. "Who are you, Jess?"

There was a long, shivering pause. He had violated her unwritten rule, not to ask questions about her background. At last she whispered, "I can't tell you that. Someday, perhaps. Not now."

There was another pause while he debated what to do. He loved her. He wanted to hold her. She was not really his, he knew. She might go away. It was the fear that lay deep-buried at the bottom of his happiness, that he might lose her. "Don't you trust me?" he asked at last.

She bent her head, exposing the soft whiteness of her nape. It was a pose that made her seem very vulnerable, very young. "I can't tell you, Philip," she repeated helplessly. "Not yet. Please don't ask me."

There was a white line around his mouth. "For how long do you think you can remain anonymous? The name of Jessica O'Neill must be familiar to every literate person in England by now. I don't know where you come from, but you are English, of that I'm sure. One day someone who knows you is going to walk into that theatre and recognize you." She winced as if he had struck her, but he continued inexorably, "You said you did not want to become famous, but you *are* famous, Jess. Your identity can't remain hidden forever."

"It doesn't need to be hidden forever," she replied quickly. "I don't plan to go on acting forever."

His face was grim. This was what he had feared. "And one day you will just disappear, back to obscurity, and Jessica O'Neill will be no more?"

"That is what I planned to do," she answered him honestly.

"And what of me, Jess? What of me?"

Slowly she raised her bent head until her eyes, wide and gray and fathomless, rested on his face. She felt as though he had a knife to her heart. For these past few days she had allowed herself to be swept along on the tide of his love, refusing to acknowledge where the sea was carrying her. There was no future for her with Philip Romney. She knew that. Once she had the money for the mortgage she would have to leave him, and the thought was terrible to her. She felt as though there were a black, deep ravine separating her from all her previous days. She knew now, now that it was too late, what it was in life that she wanted. And she could not have him. He was not for her. But she must not let him know. She must reassure him so that at least the weeks she had left would be hers. It was little enough happiness for a lifetime, she thought.

"What of you?" she repeated softly. "I said I was going to leave the stage, Philip. Not you. Not ever you. You'll have to throw me out when you want me to go."

She saw his face change at her words, his mouth taking on an expression that made her knees go weak. "I'm far more likely to chain you up," he said roughly.

At that she laughed unsteadily. "I always thought you looked like a Viking," she said, and his blue eyes glittered.

"You are a prize I mean to hold onto, my darling," he told her, and centuries of possessiveness sounded for the moment in the deep tones of his voice. She smiled but did not reply.

Linton arrived at Covent Garden about twenty minutes before the play was scheduled to begin. He paused for a short time in front of the playbill that announced the night's production, his eyes on the names listed and on one name in particular.

PLAYBILL JANUARY 28, 1815
COVENT GARDEN THEATRE

THE TRAGEDY OF
*MACBETH*

Duncan, King of Scotland, *Mr. Powell*
Macbeth, *Mr. Garreg*
Banquo, *Mr. Holland*
Macduff, *Mr. Walleck*
Malcolm, *Mr. Dawson,* Donalbain, *Mr. Palmer,*
Lennox, *Mr. Crooke,* Ross, *Mr. Fisher,* Menteith,
*Mr. Miller,* Angus, *Mr. Ray,* Caithness, *Mr. Evans,*
Fleance, *Mr. Carr,* Siward, *Mr. Maddocks,*
Young Siward, *Mr. Hughes*

Lady Macbeth, *Miss O'Neill*
Lady Macduff, *Miss Favell,*
Gentlewoman, *Mrs. Brereton*

With an inscrutable face he entered the theatre and made his way to his box. He had not wanted to ask anyone to join him but he knew his solitary presence would occasion the kind of remark he most disliked, so he had invited his cousin Bertram, Bertram's friend Sir Francis Rustington, and Lord George Litcham. The three other men were already in the box when he arrived. The theatre was filled to overflowing. "By Jove, Philip, they've all turned out to see Jessica tonight!" Bertram said enthusiastically.

Sir Francis shook his head sadly. "I don't understand it. Nice girl. Marvelous girl, really. Dash it all, how's she going to play Lady Macbeth? Woman's a horror. We had to read the play at Harrow." He shook his head again in bewilderment, and Linton smiled.

"I don't think you'll see a nice girl on the stage

tonight, Francis," he said, a flicker of irony in his voice.

"I don't know how she can do it," Bertram said with a shudder. "Imagine having to stand in front of all these people."

Jessica was feeling the tension, but not nearly as much as Lewis Garreg. No matter how the production went, Jessica O'Neill would still be Jessica O'Neill, the first actress of the London theatre. But if Lewis Garreg failed it was back to the provinces for him, back to poverty and oblivion. He wanted very much to succeed—much more than Jessica did. She stood next to him in the Green Room and when his name was called she squeezed his hand slightly. "You'll be wonderful," she said firmly. He smiled at her gratefully, took a deep breath, and headed for the stage.

Twenty minutes later her own call came. The curtain was down as the scenery was being changed and she took her place on center stage, a letter in her hands. She wore a black velvet gown of medieval cut. Her hair was loosely pulled off her face and coiled on her neck. She stood perfectly still, no expression on her face, and the curtain slowly began to rise. At the sight of her, standing solitary in the middle of the wide stage, the theatre erupted.

Her eyes looked out into the auditorium toward the cheering throng. They passed over the professional men jammed uncomfortably together on benches in the pit, over the aristocrats in the boxes, up to the vast reaches of the gallery where sat the people. Gradually the noise died away and she bent her eyes to the paper she was holding. "They met me in the day of success," she began, her deep clear, resonant voice perfectly audible throughout the theatre.

She went through the speech faultlessly, as Linton, who was mentally reciting it with her, was aware. She finished and the messenger came on with news of the king's arrival. With the entrance of the messenger something clicked in Jessica's mind and she had it at last, that total and undistracted concentration on the character she was portraying that she had sought so vainly this last week. The theatre, the audience, Linton . . . everything fell away from her but the words she was to say. The messenger exited and she lifted her face, beautiful and bright and pitiless, and slowly, with terrible intensity, she began Lady Macbeth's powerful invocation to the evil spirits. When she had finished the atmosphere in the theatre was electric and Lewis Garreg, coming on stage, met, not the Jessica he had been rehearsing with all week, but a bright angel who fixed on him eyes of possession and passion and desire.

"My dearest love," his rich, beautifully flexible voice matched hers in power. He held her close for a moment, then looked down unflinchingly into her face. "Duncan comes here tonight."

As the act progressed Linton looked around the theatre. It was deathly silent, not a cough, not a rustle of paper or of silk was to be heard. The full attention of the hundreds of spectators was trained on the stage, on the duel that was being fought between Macbeth's better nature and his wife, between Lewis Garreg, who was turning in a magnificent performance, and Jessica.

He looked back to the stage. Garreg had turned away from her, his jaw set stubbornly.

> Prithee peace!
> I dare do all that may become a man.
> Who dares do more is none.

He walked to a bench on stage left and sat down, his eyes brooding upon the ground. There was a long silence as Jessica regarded him, and then she exploded into passion and anger.

> What beast was't then
> That made you break this enterprise to me?

Slowly she walked across the stage until she stood before him. She put her hands on his shoulders. He raised his head, and her gray eyes, burning and intent in her proud, determined face, held his relentlessly.

> I have given suck, and know
> How tender 'tis to love the babe that milks me

She paused and then went on, no anger in her voice now. It was clear and cold and truthful.

> I would, while it was smiling in my face,
> Have plucked my nipple from his boneless gums
> 'And dashed the brains out, had I so sworn
> as you
> Have done to this.

Beside him Linton could hear the shocked intake of Bertram's breath. Lord George's knuckles were white as he gripped the front of the box. On the stage Garreg began to waver.

> If we should fail?

An enchanting smile lit Jessica's face.

> We fail?
> But screw your courage to the sticking place,
> And we'll not fail.

The tension in the theatre was thick and palpable. On stage the last of Macbeth's objections fell and his own ambition answered forth to his wife's. They stood together, two passionate, proud people in the intensity of their fixed purpose, their two young, formidable faces looking for the moment strangely alike. When the curtain came down on Act I there was at least one full minute of stunned silence before the applause began.

The remainder of the play was of the same caliber. There wasn't a person present at that performance who didn't remember it vividly for the rest of his life: the first and only time Jessica O'Neill played Lady

Macbeth. Lewis Garreg would play Macbeth many more times, and he always gave a powerful, moving performance, but never again would there be that electricity in the air, that knowledge that one was watching what the *Morning Post* would call the next day "one of the finest pieces of acting we have ever beheld, or perhaps that the stage has ever known."

# Chapter Fifteen

> . . . and all things keep
> Time with the season; only she doth carry
> June in her eyes, in her heart January.
> —THOMAS CAREW

After the performance Linton found Jessica in the Green Room. She was standing with Lewis Garreg, introducing him to the famous and the great who were thronging to congratulate her. Linton watched her in silence for a moment from the doorway. It was Garreg's night as well as hers; her demeanor made that clear. The young man was obviously both exhilarated and nervous. He had never met so many members of the nobility in his life. With some amusement Linton thought that he was clinging to Jessica as if she were a lifeline.

Her head turned, and across the room their eyes met. Lord George, standing next to Linton, intercepted that look and, startled, turned to his friend. What he saw for a brief unguarded moment on Linton's face made his heart begin to pound. It couldn't be, he thought involuntarily. *What* couldn't be, another part of his mind asked objectively as he followed Linton across the floor. Lord George did not answer himself. He only knew he was conscious of a wish that Lady

Maria Selsey was not indisposed at the moment. He had a horrible sinking feeling that Linton was in deeper than was safe and might very well have to be rescued.

Jessica, unaware that she had alarmed Lord George, greeted him with friendliness. And she laughed at Bertram when he said, "You scared me to death, Jessica!"

"Indeed you did," a smooth voice said next to her elbow, and she turned to find Lord Alden looking at her with a mixture of speculation and desire that she found peculiarly repulsive.

"Did I, my lord?" she asked stiffly.

He smiled and her eyes narrowed. Bertram's attention had been momentarily distracted, and for a brief minute she and Lord Alden might have been alone. "Linton can't possibly appreciate a woman like you," he said softly.

"And you think you can?" Her voice expressed nothing but a kind of wary contempt.

"I am sure of it." His voice hardened. "Whatever he is giving you, I'll double it."

Slowly she shook her head. "No, you won't," she said, and now her voice was under its familiar control, aloof and contained. Linton put a hand on her shoulder and she turned back to him with relief.

"I've asked Mr. Garreg to accompany us to a champagne supper at the Grillon. Some of the rest of the cast are coming and a few of my own friends."

She smiled with genuine pleasure. "Thank you, Philip. This is really Lewis's triumph, you know."

"No, it is not," he replied soberly. "Garreg was

**119**

marvelous, that I agree. But you were more than that. And you know it."

Her lips curved a little, but she made no reply. In fact she said nothing about the performance until the large company was seated around a table in the Grillon's private dining room and toasts were being made. "To many more performances like the one we saw tonight," said Thomas Harris, raising his champagne glass to Jessica and Lewis Garreg. After the toast was drunk Jessica got to her feet.

"I thank you very much, all of you, for your kind words. I have an announcement to make that I am afraid will make some of you unhappy. Tonight was my last performance. I am retiring from the theatre."

Cries of protest and of incredulity rose from every pair of lips. Of all the table only Jessica and Linton remained silent. She sat down, impervious to the noise and the pleas around her, aware only of the man who sat so quietly at the opposite end of the long table. He was looking at the tablecloth in front of him as if it contained the answer to a secret he had long wanted to unlock. Finally, aware of her gaze, he looked up, and the sudden lift and turn of his head was as direct as a touch. Her face relaxed a little and he raised a reassuring eyebrow.

"I will not change my mind," she said then.

"But *why?*" Thomas Harris almost wailed. "For God's sake, Jessica, *why?*"

"I am tired of acting," she said simply. "I don't want to do it any more."

He stared at her with first exasperation, then incredulity, then astonishment. She meant it. Jessica

O'Neill, who had all of London at her feet, was leaving the theatre. And he thought he knew why. He directed his gaze, filled with reproach, at the Earl of Linton.

Linton's face was inscrutable. With seemingly little effort he got the upset dinner party back on its proper path again, although it was distinctly more subdued than it had been before Jessica's announcement.

It had been raining steadily all evening, and while they had been at supper the rain had turned to sleet. Jessica and Linton made a dash for the carriage. She had the hood of her velvet cloak pulled over her head. His head was bare and once they were safely inside the carriage she cast a reproachful look toward it, unmistakably bright in the darkness next to her. "You are going to contract pneumonia one day the way you go around bareheaded in all sorts of weather. It isn't even fashionable."

"A little damp isn't going to hurt me," he said with slow amusement.

She raised her hand to his hair. "That is not a little damp," she said severely.

"If I contract pneumonia you will have the pleasure of saying, 'I told you so,' " he replied serenely.

She leaned back and looked at him, but he was only a shadow in the darkness of the coach. "When I first met you I thought you were the most gentle, patient, good-natured man I had ever known. You are also, I have since discovered, obstinate as a pig."

"What an odd simile," he mused thoughtfully.

"Why, I wonder, should pigs be more obstinate than other animals?"

Reluctantly she laughed. "You are impossible."

"My sister tells me I am spoiled rotten," he said in a detached, objective tone.

"You are," she agreed cordially. "And I have no doubt your sister is partly to blame."

He reached out and took her hand. "No. She blames it all on my mother." He pulled her toward him, then slid an arm around her shoulders. Her hood slipped back and his lips found the warm spot just below her ear where he knew she liked to be kissed. "Will you spoil me, Jess?" he murmured.

"Why not?" she whispered in reply. "The damage is already done."

They got back to Montpelier Square at about two in the morning. Jessica had told her maid not to wait up for her, so Linton undid the hooks of her dress. She stepped out of it, smoothed its silk folds, and went to hang it in the wardrobe. He took his own coat off and laid it on a chair. "You gave the finest performance I have ever seen tonight," he said as he slowly undid his shirt. "Are you quite sure you won't miss the stage?"

She took the pins out of her hair. "Quite sure."

There was silence in the room; the only sounds were the crackling of her brush as she pulled it through her loosened hair and the sleet pelting against the window. "Why, Jess?" he said at last. "Why did you do it?"

She thought for a minute, her head bent a little, her

brow grave. "I have been thinking of what you said earlier, about the likelihood of someone recognizing me. And the reasons I gave to Mr. Harris are also true. I enjoyed doing *Macbeth* tonight. I'm glad I did it well. But I don't want to do it again."

"You won't miss it?" he asked again.

She turned on the dressing table chair until she was facing him. His hair was ruffled from her hand, his eyes the intense blue emotion always turned them. "What are you worried about, Philip?" she asked, real puzzlement in her voice. "Do you think I'm going to pine away once I'm removed from the excitement and the applause?"

"Something like that," he replied evenly.

She smiled a litle wryly. "All my life I have been a rather solitary person. I grew up in the country. I am not accustomed to being surrounded by a great number of people. I won't miss it."

"Would you like to live in the country again, Jess?" he asked, and his voice was deadly serious.

She looked at him and her heart ached. He would give her whatever she wanted. She knew that. If she said she wanted to race horses he would buy her a stud. If she wanted to live in the country he would buy her an estate. He would give her anything, except what she wanted most of all. He could not give her that. Any chance she ever had of sharing a normal life with him was gone, irrevocably. She was Jessica O'Neill. An actress. His mistress. There was no way in the world she could ever become his wife. So she smiled around the pain and said, "For now I am happy as I am."

123

He came and knelt before her. "You will stay here with me?"

She cupped his face between her hands. "Yes."

"I have an idea for the future. Will you trust me to work it out for us?"

"Yes," she said again. She looked into his face, held so lightly between her two hands. "I plan to keep myself very busy," she said softly.

"What are you going to do?"

"Spoil you," she returned, her mouth curving tenderly.

His face took on a look she recognized and her heart began to race. "Are you now?" he said. His hands came up to cover hers and move them to his mouth.

"Yes," Her eyes were held, drowning, in his.

He kissed the palms of her hands. "Good." He rose and pulled her unresisting body up, effortlessly, into his arms. "Then let's go to bed," he said, and once again, with eyes closed this time, she said,

"Yes."

# Chapter Sixteen

Yet therein now doth lodge a noble Peer,
Great England's glory, and the world's wide
wonder,

—EDMUND SPENSER

Three weeks later Linton took Jessica with him to dinner at Holland House. Lord Holland had long been one of his favorite friends and whenever Linton was in London he invariably spent a good deal of time at the stately red brick Jacobean mansion in Kensington. The most remarkable men of the time were often to be found crowded around the dinner table at Holland House. There one could find statesmen, writers, artists, and distinguished foreigners. Holland House was the intellectual center of the Whig culture that was Linton's heritage. He enjoyed evenings in the long library, where flourished vigorous and cultivated discussions that could pass from politics to history, from history to literature, with a freedom and intellectual depth to be found nowhere else in England.

Holland House was the only one of the houses he usually visited to which Linton felt he could bring Jessica. Many of the ladies in the highest of London society were notably promiscuous, but there was a subtle line between what society condoned and what it condemned. Jessica had crossed that line when she went on the stage.

Lady Holland, however, was another person who had violated society's rules of decorum. She was a divorced woman. She had run away from her first husband, Sir Godfrey Webster, and had lived with Lord Holland openly before her divorce became final. Although she was hostess to some of the most brilliant gatherings in Europe, she was still not received by the most rigid ladies who ruled the ton. So the rule for an invitation to Holland House was talent, genius, and wit, not social status.

When Linton had asked her if he might bring Jessica she had looked surprised at first but then she readily agreed. The high-handed bossy manner she adopted with most people was noticeably softened whenever Lady Holland spoke to Linton. "By all means, Linton," she had said cordially. "Lord Holland and I shall be happy to have such a brilliant addition to our company."

Lady Holland's surprise was slight compared to Jessica's when Linton told her of the invitation. "You can't be serious," she said incredulously. "I can't go there."

"Why not? You are invited."

"But I'm an *actress*, Philip. I can't be received by society."

"You are not an actress any longer," he replied. "I want you to meet Lord Holland. He is one of my dearest friends. And he wants to meet you. So where is the difficulty?"

"I can't go," she repeated.

"You are going," he said flatly. His jaw was set in a way she had seen only once or twice before. There was a tense pause.

"All right," she capitulated faintly, a trifle bewildered to find herself so helpless and pliant before his determination.

He smiled, his eyes warm with approval. "Good. You'll surprise yourself and have a good time. I promise you."

He was right. Jessica had never experienced anything quite like Holland House. The dining room table was jammed and she ate as best she could, her arms glued to her sides. At one point Lady Holland loudly demanded that Mr. Parkinson change places with Mr. Rogers and both gentlemen complied with much good-natured grumbling. Jessica sat at Lord Holland's right, and her initial nervousness disappeared quite soon under the influence of his infectious good humor.

They spoke about Linton, who was jammed in halfway down the table from them. "It is a pity Philip is so uninterested in politics," Lord Holland said to her. "Lord Grey and I have been trying for years to get him to take a hand, with little success I might add."

"Do you and Philip agree on politics, my lord?" Jessica asked cautiously. She did not think Linton was uninterested in the subject. She did know that Lord Holland headed the Foxite faction of the Whig party. He and Lord Grey had dedicated themselves to the preservation of the ideas and policies of Charles James Fox, who also happened to be Lord Holland's uncle. Charles Fox, however, had been dead for six years, and the world had changed considerably since his demise. Linton might love Lord Holland as a friend but Jessica did not think he loved his friend's politics.

"We have a few minor disagreements," Lord Holland assured her cheerfully. "Philip's concern for his agricultural workers sometimes overbalances his native good sense. But then Lord Grey and I certainly are in favor of reform. There can be little disagreement on that issue."

"I should think not," Jessica murmured quietly.

He raised his black, bushy eyebrows. "Are you a reformer too, Miss O'Neill?"

"I grew up in the country, my lord, so I am aware of the hardships country people are facing these days. The Corn Laws benefit the landowner and large farmer at the expense of everybody else. Farm laborers who are fortunate enough to have an employer like Philip have cottages and gardens where they can grow their own vegetables and keep a pig and some chickens. Those who are not so fortunate live marginal existences on bread, butter, and half-rotten potatoes."

Lord Holland was nodding in agreement. "It is disgraceful, certainly, and all too often the result of cits and commercials buying estates and trying to set themselves up as landed gentry. The country is filled with nabobs, contractors, commissioners, loan-jobbers, retired generals and admirals. They have no care for their own people, as we do. Take Philip for example. He is a nobleman who lives up to his title. He has a great sense of responsibility toward those beneath him or in his charge and he wholeheartedly protects the people who work for him. He is just, charitable, and generous. To want to hand the government of the country from *him* to the likes of a manufacturer from Yorkshire is what I have no patience with."

Jessica gently pointed out that the country was not governed by Philip and his like but by diehard Tories, led by Lord Liverpool, who were adamantly opposed to change of any sort.

"Quite right," replied Lord Holland instantly. "That is why we need Philip to take an active hand in unseating the Tories."

"Why Philip?" she asked.

"Everybody likes him so much," replied Lord Holland promptly. "I hardly know anyone of whom everyone entertains so favorable an opinion."

She smiled at Lord Holland, a flicker of irony in her gray eyes. "Are you asking me to be your recruiter, Lord Holland?"

He smiled easily back, full of the charm and bonhomie that made him so lovable. "Why not, Miss O'Neill? Why not?"

Jessica and Linton drove home late that evening. He was very pleased. He had had ulterior motives for wishing Jessica to venture out to Holland House, and the evening had been a resounding success. Before they left Lady Holland had called him over to her and said in a low voice, "How serious is this, Linton?"

He had laughed, the firelight calling forth sparks of blue from his narrowed eyes. "Very serious," he had said.

"So. She is an unusual girl." There was a little

129

silence as she continued to look at him. Then she said, "She will always be welcome here."

He took her hand. "Thank you, ma'am." He was very grave now. "We may have need of a friend."

She nodded decisively. "You have one in me. And in Lord Holland as well."

He was thinking of this exchange now as he said to Jessica, "You and Lord Holland seemed to get along like a house on fire."

"What a nice man he is!" she replied warmly.

"He is. What did you talk about?"

"You." Laughter hovered in the corners of her mouth. "He wants me to convince you to go in for politics."

"Oh Lord," he groaned.

"He said lovely things about you."

"He wouldn't say them if he knew my true thoughts about his politics."

"And what are your true thoughts?"

"The Whigs are hopeless at the moment," he said brutally. "There are factions within factions. First there are the Grenvillites, who are just like the Tories only they think Lord Grenville should be prime minister and not old Liverpool. Then there are the Foxites. Did Holland tell you he was in favor of reform?"

She nodded.

"Of course. Just don't ever ask him to put theory into practice. Besides, the Foxites have no use for economics and economics is, of course, the whole point of reform. Then there are the reformers, people like Whitbread and young Grey and Brougham. But they all disagree with each other as well as with the Grenvillites and the Foxites."

"Heavens. It seems as though the opposition party is in opposition to itself."

"The problem is they can discover nothing on which they can agree to unite in opposition."

"Have you spoken to Lord Holland about this?"

He shrugged. "What's the point, Jess? If there were a party for me to join, I'd join it; but it's either the Whigs or the Tories, and I certainly can't become a Tory!"

"But perhaps Lord Holland and the others could agree to compromise?"

He snorted. "Holland and Grey make it a point of honor not to work with anyone they disagree with about anything."

"Oh."

"Precisely. So I keep my mouth pretty well shut. All these people happen to be my friends, you see, and I do like them enormously."

"The world is changing despite them, Philip," she said. "As you once told me, England is turning from an agricultural to a manufacturing country. The economic power is no longer solely in the hands of the landowners. The new holders of the country's wealth, those manufacturers and nabobs Lord Holland spoke so scornfully about, are going to demand their share of the political power as well."

"Of course. And they will get it, eventually. In the meantime I'll just continue to farm."

She reached out and took his hand. "You are one of a rare breed, my lord, do you know that?"

"What breed?" he asked.

"You are a genuinely independent man," she answered. "And I love you."

Linton had bought Jessica a horse, and they had formed the habit of rising early and riding in Hyde Park. There was no one around to frown at them as they galloped hard through the cold February mornings, their breaths hanging white on the chill air. They would return to Montpelier Square, cheeks glowing, to consume an enormous breakfast and to plan their day.

The morning after the dinner at Holland House was no exception to their usual routine, a routine that had all the sanctity of three weeks of practice. They were sitting in the dining room over breakfast when a decided break in that routine occurred. Peter entered the room and said woodenly, "Sir Matthew Selsey to see you, my lord."

Surprise flickered in Linton's eyes. "Show him in here."

"Very good, my lord."

Linton turned to Jessica. "My brother-in-law," he said briefly.

"I'll go." She rose from her seat, but he reached out and his fingers clamped hard on her wrist. "No. I want you to stay." She couldn't pull away from him without a struggle, and there was the sound of steps in the hallway. There was a spark of anger in her clear gray eyes but she sat down. He released her wrist as his brother-in-law came into the room.

"Matt!" He rose and held out his hand. "I didn't even know you were in the country. How is Maria?"

Sir Matthew Selsey was a pleasant-looking man in his middle forties, with brown hair and surprisingly vivid hazel eyes. He took Linton's hand. "I am happy to tell you you have a new niece," he said, his face breaking into a grin.

"Congratulations!" Linton sounded delighted. "Another girl after all those boys. And how is Maria?"

"Fine. I only arrived home a week ago, and she had the baby the next day. It was all the excitement of my unexpected arrival, she said."

Linton laughed, then he turned to Jessica. "I beg your pardon, Jess, but good news often makes me forget my manners. May I present my brother-in-law, Sir Matthew Selsey. Miss Jessica O'Neill, Matt."

Jessica's face wore its aloof, guarded expression, but Sir Matthew smiled at her warmly. "How do you do, Miss O'Neill. Forgive me for breaking in upon you so rudely."

"It is quite all right," she replied. "Will you sit down, Sir Matthew, and have some breakfast?"

"I'll have a cup of coffee, gladly."

He sat down across from her, and Linton said, "I didn't know you were coming back to England."

"I wasn't, originally," Sir Matthew replied, stirring his coffee, "but I found myself getting more and more worried about Maria. This may be our sixth child but after all she *is* thirty-eight even if she doesn't look it. And it has been six years since John." His eyes suddenly twinkled. "Don't ever tell her I said that, Philip."

"I wouldn't dare." They both laughed. "What are you doing in London, Matt?"

"I had to see Castlereagh. I've been in London two days and I'm going back to Selsey this afternoon. Unfortunately I must leave for Vienna next week. Maria and the children will join me in April."

"Have you been staying in Grosvenor Square?"

"Yes."

"Ah." Linton's eyes, full of blue light, rested thoughtfully on his brother-in-law's face.

Sir Matthew's expression remained placid; he was, after all, a diplomat. He turned to Jessica. "Linton's man gave me your direction. I shouldn't have come barging in if I hadn't been so short of time." He gave her his warm smile. "I did want to break the good news myself."

Jessica looked back and then her thin, grave face lit with an answering smile. "Of course you did. It is not every day one has a new daughter. What are you calling her?"

Matt grinned. "The boys wanted to name her Hortense."

Jessica's rich, deep laugh rippled. "Aren't boys wretched?"

"Jess should know," Linton said, amusement in his own voice. "She has two brothers about Matthew's and Lawrence's ages. What name *did* you decide on, Matt?"

"Elizabeth Maria Deborah."

"That's lovely," Jessica said.

"It is my mother's name," Linton told her with a pleased smile.

Sir Matthew stayed for perhaps twenty more minutes, and when he left Linton saw him to the door.

"I can see why you aren't spending your time in Grosvenor Square, Philip," his brother-in-law said. "She is lovely. And—unusual."

"Unusual. That was Lady Holland's word also."

Sir Matthew looked startled. "Lady Holland! Have you taken her to Holland House then?"

"Yes."

Sir Matthew looked at Linton's face and said no more. They shook hands and parted the good friends they had always been. Linton walked back to the dining room where Jessica still sat. "Maria will have it all out of him in half an hour," he said. "Come into the drawing room. I have to talk to you."

# Chapter Seventeen

What is love? 'Tis not hereafter,
Present mirth hath present laughter,
What's to come is still unsure.
—WILLIAM SHAKESPEARE

Linton's absence from Grosvenor Square had been noticed by people other than Sir Matthew Selsey. A number of friends, missing him at the club, had called at Linton House to be informed by a wooden-faced butler that "Lord Linton is not in." Nor, it appeared, was he expected.

Lord George Litcham was one of the first to take serious alarm. He had spent as much time as anyone in the company of Linton and Jessica, and he was not insensitive. After a great deal of thought he broached the matter to Bertram Romney.

"Worried about Philip?" said that young man. "I don't understand you, Litcham. Dash it all, Jessica isn't one of those avaricious harpies who take a man for all he's worth. And even if she were it wouldn't matter. Linton is too rich to be fleeced like that."

"I know she isn't one of that breed, Romney," replied Lord George. "That is precisely what worries me. She is different. *They* are different." He hesitated. "I am very much afraid Linton is serious about her."

136

"Serious?"

Lord George said patiently, like a man talking to a very small child, "I am afraid he means to marry her."

Bertram's eyes widened. "He couldn't."

"I don't know," Lord George said slowly.

There was a very long silence. "We need my cousin, Maria Selsey," Bertram finally said. "She scares me half to death, but she'll know what to do."

"I thought Lady Maria was expecting a child any day now."

"Burn it, so she is! Isn't that just like a woman? As soon as she has a chance to make herself useful she's indisposed."

"What about Lady Linton?" Lord George asked, ignoring Bertram's strictures on the opposite sex.

Bertram looked unhappy. "Dash it all, my Aunt Elizabeth thinks the sun rises and sets on Linton's head. What am I to do? Write and tell her he is in danger of marrying his mistress? Which I'm not at all sure he is, by the way." There was a little silence as Bertram looked at the paper lying on his table. "Besides, she's a first-rate girl, Jess. I like her."

"I know," said Lord George. "So do I. And that, Romney, is the problem."

In the end they decided that Bertram would write a letter to his own mother asking her to come up to town for a week or two. "Very sensible woman, my mother," Bertram had assured Lord George. "She likes Philip. If he needs rescuing she'll be glad to lend her assistance. I'm sure of it."

\*     \*     \*

.Others were not so considerate of the delicate state of Lady Maria or the fond motherly heart of Lady Linton. Both of these ladies received missives from various friends who were staying in London at present and who found Linton's behavior sufficiently ödd to inspire a report to his womenfolk. At first they had shrugged off the letters as gossip, then they had been angry, finally they became alarmed.

"Look at this, mother," Maria said two mornings before her baby was born. "A letter from Emily Cowper."

"About Philip?" asked Lady Linton, anxiety in her voice.

"Not *about* Philip. Emily is too polite for that. She merely *mentions* Philip, but her comments are very much to the point."

They were sitting in the morning parlor at Selsey Place, and now Lady Linton laid down her pen and put aside the letter she had been writing. "What does she say?"

"I saw Linton yesterday," Maria read. "It was a wretched, rainy day but I had to go to Worth's for a fitting and as I was on my way home I passed him and Miss O'Neill as they were coming out of the park. They had evidently been riding in the rain, something I wouldn't do if my life depended upon it. But they were both laughing—even with water streaming down their faces! He is as handsome as ever, Maria, even waterlogged. I don't see him at all socially, so perhaps you can write to ascertain if he has caught pneumonia or not." Maria looked up. "Then she goes on to something else." She closed the letter. "I don't like it, mother. Emily would not have written to me if she hadn't thought I should know what is going on."

"But what *is* going on, Maria?" asked Lady Linton. "Philip has a mistress. He has had mistresses before and no one got upset like this."

"He is living with her," Maria said slowly. "Evidently he is never at Grosvenor Square. And you heard what Emily Cowper wrote. He isn't going out socially. From what I can gather he spends all his time with this actress."

"But what can we do?" asked Lady Linton.

"I think you should go up to London, mother," Lady Maria said decisively.

But Lady Linton refused to leave her daughter at such a critical time, and the next day Sir Matthew Selsey came home. In the end he was the one charged with "finding out what Philip is up to."

Sir Matthew had not been overly pleased about his commission. He had a great deal of liking and an equally great deal of respect for his brother-in-law and was quite positive that jealous gossip was at the root of all the reports that had been reaching Selsey Place. But he had to go up to London anyway, so he placated his wife by assuring her that he would look into the matter.

After two days at Grosvenor Square he had not been so sanguine. Then he had a conversation with Bertram's mother, a woman whose good sense he had always respected. The fact that Bertram, a careless young scamp if ever he saw one, had seen fit to call in his mother sounded an alarm to Sir Matthew immediately. An alarm Mrs. Romney herself did little to soften.

"He is getting himself talked about," Mrs. Romney said frankly. "And that is something Linton never did before. You can see them frequently at the opera and at the theatre. Of course he can't take her into good company, but neither does he take her into the sort of company she *could* frequent." She raised her eyes and looked at Sir Matthew very soberly. They were seated in the drawing room of the house of Lady Marchmain, Mrs. Romney's sister with whom Mrs. Romney was staying during this brief visit to London. She had written asking Sir Matthew to visit her as soon as she had heard he was in town. "I've met her," she said to him now.

He said nothing, but his brows rose a trifle.

"At the opera," she replied to his silent query. "I made Bertram take me to their box."

"My dear ma'am!" protested Sir Matthew.

"Oh, we were very discreet," Mrs. Romney assured him. "We all stood at the back of the box, almost in the corridor."

"What did Philip do when you appeared?"

"I think he was glad to see me. He introduced Miss O'Neill immediately."

"Did he?" said Sir Matthew slowly. "And what did you think of her, ma'am?"

"She's striking. And well-bred. And proud. And there is something very serious between her and Linton."

He frowned. "How can you say that?"

"It's hard to explain, Matthew, but I am not mistaken." She frowned a little herself in the effort to explain what she meant. "Linton was charming—you know how he can be when he exerts himself. And she was pleasant, if a little reserved. But I felt almost as if I were intruding. Not because they didn't want to see me. I told you earlier I think Linton was glad of an opportunity to introduce her. But it is as if the bond between them is so strong that it keeps everyone else at a distance, even though they don't mean it to."

Sir Matthew had come away from Lady Marchmain's considerably perturbed. It was his conversation with Mrs. Romney that had precipitated his descent on Montpelier Square. It was a visit that left him, if possible, even more concerned.

It took, in fact, forty-five minutes for Lady Maria to elicit the main reasons for Sir Matthew's concern.

"He took her to Holland House?" she asked incredulously.

"I've already told you that, Maria."

"And introduced her to Catherine Romney?"

"Yes."

Maria was reclining on a chaise longue in her bedroom, and she had moved her legs aside to make room for her husband to sit. Her pale hair was tied loosely back from her face and she wore a foamy sea green negligee. She most emphatically did not look thirty-eight years old. "What do you think, Matt?" she asked now directly.

"I think Philip is in love with this girl," he answered gravely.

There was a pause. "Damn!" said Lady Maria.

"Yes."

Her green eyes narrowed. "You don't think he is planning anything foolish?"

He shook his head. "I don't know. She is an extraordinary girl, Maria. A person to be reckoned with."

"How does she feel about him?"

He smiled a little crookedly. "Can you imagine any woman, however extraordinary, who could resist your brother when he sets out to charm?"

"Oh dear," she said in a suddenly small voice.

"And of course it is much more than that," he went on. "He made it very clear how he expected her to be treated. He was completely pleasant but he was there, like a rock, between her and any possible familiarity or insult." He sighed a little wearily. "I had no idea what the diplomatic corps was missing in Philip."

"He can't possibly mean to marry her?" said Maria in a horrified voice.

"I don't know what he means, my love," replied her husband. "But I certainly wouldn't rule it out."

# Chapter Eighteen

But ah, to kiss and then to part!—
How deep it struck, speak, gods, you know
Kisses make men loath to go.
                        —THOMAS CAMPION

Jessica was unaware of the furor her relationship with
Linton was causing in the breasts of his family and
friends. She had too many other things on her mind.

At first, after her final appearance in *Macbeth,* she
had just relaxed and given herself up to the joy of
being with him. It was too constant a pain to be con-
tinually dwelling on the inevitable future, so she shut
it out and lost herself in the richness of her union with
him. It was so sweet and satisfying to be with him, to
love and to know herself loved in return. There had
never been anyone to whom she could talk as she
talked to him. And when they were silent it was the
comfortable, sustaining silence of deep intimacy, a
silence that was sometimes more communicative than
words.

But this cocoonlike state of mind could not last. On
February 4 she got a statement from her bank saying
her monthly allowance had been paid into her account. She sat in front of the desk where she kept her
accounts and looked at her figures. With a bitter, sear-

ing pain in her heart she realized that she had the mortgage money. The next month's allowance would pay the interest. Winchcombe would be clear and she could go home. She would have to go home.

For a short time she sat at the desk, eyes closed, wishing uselessly, hopelessly, achingly, that she had not. But she could not stay on here indefinitely as Linton's mistress. She had the boys to consider. And herself. She had felt morally justified to do what she was doing because of her dire necessity. Once that necessity was removed her actions would have to be viewed in quite another light and she wasn't sure if she could face up to the picture that would be presented to her then.

There was also a final and overriding fact that made her leaving him an absolute necessity. She was sure she was with child.

When she had missed her menses at the end of December she had not been greatly concerned. She had missed occasionally before and had always assumed it was because of the hard, active life she led. She was working hard in the theatre as well. She had not been overly disturbed. She had had faith in Mrs. Brereton's herbs.

Then she missed in January as well. She had never gone two months before. And her breasts were larger and very tender. With a tightness of fear in her chest she realized what the probable cause of these symptoms was.

Her first reaction had been panic. She had heard talk among the actresses she worked with. There was probably something she could do about getting rid of it.

But the more she thought about it the more impossible such a course of action became. What am I going to do with it? one part of her mind asked. How am I going to explain? But—a child, the other part answered. Philip's child. And her hand went, unconsciously, to her stomach. I may lose Philip, but I will have his child, she thought. And suddenly, fiercely, she knew she wanted this child, would fight to keep it. I can tell them at home that I was married, she thought. I'll think of some story. They still won't need to know the truth.

Nor could she tell the truth to Linton. She didn't know what he would do but she was quite sure he would do something. She didn't want the status quo upset. She wanted her last month with him. She wanted her memories that would have to last her for a very long time. For the rest of her life, in fact.

And then he took her to Holland House. And the next morning Sir Matthew Selsey came to Montpelier Square. And Linton said, "Come into the drawing room. I have to talk to you."

She went with him, a puzzled look in her eyes. But she obediently sat down on the sofa he indicated, folded her hands in her lap, and gazed up at him as he stood before the mantel.

He looked tense. A muscle flickered once in the angle of his jaw, and she frowned. "What is it, Philip?"

"Jess." His voice was deeper than usual. "How much do you love me?"

She looked at him in silence for a moment, her large eyes steady on the cleanly sculptured face she knew better than her own. "If you don't know the answer to that question by now you never will," she answered quietly at last.

"I want you to marry me," he said.

There was a moment of stunned silence before she answered. "What did you say?" She sounded as if the breath had been knocked out of her.

He crossed the room to kneel before her, taking her cold hand in his two large, warm ones and looking compellingly into her eyes. "I want you to marry me," he repeated.

She closed her eyes so he should not see the longing she knew must be there. "It is not possible," she breathed.

"Why not?" She did not answer, and he held her hand more tightly. "Look at me, Jess!" he said strongly. "Why not?"

Her eyes opened. She ran her tongue over lips that were suddenly dry. She looked into the face she loved and her heart began to slam in slow painful strokes. His eyes were intensely blue, brimming with a fierce purpose that frightened her. "We can live at Staplehurst," he said. "You won't have to come to London if you don't want to. You'll like Staplehurst. And we shall be together."

Weakly, she shook her head. "You would be disgraced if you married me. What of your mother? Your sister? They would be horrified. They must be wondering already. That is why they sent Sir Matthew, isn't it?" He didn't answer, and she went on. "You don't even know who I am."

"I don't care who you are." His voice was quiet but there was a note in it Jessica recognized. She shivered, feeling herself bending to his will, vulnerable and disarmed as only he could leave her. She needed time to think. She knew what she wanted to do. She had to decide what it was she ought to do. She made a small negative movement with her head and he said, "I love you."

"Philip." She leaned forward and pressed her face against the hardness of his shoulder. He locked his arms tightly around her body and held her to him.

"Marry me, Jess," he said softly.

"I need to think about it," she said, her voice muffled.

His jaw tightened, but his voice remained quiet. "Don't think for too long, will you?"

She stayed where she was, her body pressed tightly against his. "No," she said. "I love you."

"I know you do," he answered. "The thing to keep in mind is that I feel the same way about you."


At Selsey Place Lady Maria held a council of war with her husband and her mother. "You say Philip took her to Holland House?" Lady Linton asked her son-in-law.

"Yes."

"And Catherine Romney says she is worried," put in Lady Maria. "Mother, you must go up to London! It simply isn't like Philip to behave like this."

"No. It is not like him at all," replied Lady Linton. There was a faint line between her delicate brows. "I have made it a rule never to interfere in Philip's affairs, but I think this time is different. I will go up to London."

"When?" asked her daughter.

"Tomorrow morning," said Lady Linton. "If you will excuse me I'll tell Weber to pack."

At about the same time that Lady Maria was speaking to her husband and mother, Mrs. Romney received a note that surprised her greatly. "Could you possibly meet me in one hour's time at the British Museum?" it read. "There is something of great importance that I must discuss with you. I shall be looking at the Townley collection. Jessica O'Neill."

An hour and fifteen minutes later Mrs. Romney came up to Jessica as she stood gazing intently at a Greek statue. "Miss O'Neill?" she said in her quiet, cultured voice.

Jessica's head turned quickly. Her cheeks flushed, then went very pale. 'Thank you for coming." The room was empty, and Jessica gestured to a bench along one of the walls. "If you will be seated for a few moments I will tell you why I asked you to come."

Mrs. Romney moved obediently to the proffered seat and Jessica sat down next to her. "I need some advice," she said, her eyes fixed straight ahead of her. "Lord Linton has asked me to marry him." She spoke in a low, steady voice; her hands were clasped tightly together in her lap.

Mrs. Romney felt as though a bolt of lightning had

just shot through her. It was one thing to entertain certain fears and quite another to have them so baldly confirmed. Catherine Romney had a deep affection for Lord Linton's mother and a great deal of respect for Linton himself. She resolved to do what she could to save him from this disastrously unwise marriage he had evidently set himself on. She looked at Jessica. "And what have you answered him?" she asked cautiously.

"I told him I needed time to think about it." Jessica's gray eyes were dark as they turned to regard Mrs. Romney gravely. "He has told me that a marriage between us is possible. I have come to you to ask if that is so."

There was a moment's silence as Mrs. Romney looked consideringly at Jessica. Her first thought had been that the girl wanted money, but now she was not so sure. It was entirely possible that what she had said was true, that her answer to Linton would depend on what Mrs. Romney told her. "If you love him," she said flatly, her eyes holding the gray ones of the girl, "you will not marry him."

Jessica's eyes fell. "I see," she said quietly.

"I wonder if you do. If you marry him it will bring inexpressible dismay to all those who are bound to him by ties of blood. You will rob him of all his friends and degrade him in the eyes of his peers. If you love him you will not subject him to such a sorrow."

It was a full minute before Jessica replied and when she did her voice was perfectly normal. "You may put your mind at rest, Mrs. Romney. I will not marry him to have him disgraced and rejected by his own people." She turned her proud head toward the woman seated next to her. "Thank you for coming and for your advice. It was not unexpected."

Catherine Romney looked back at the carefully shuttered face of the girl Linton loved. "I am sorry, my dear." She spoke quite gently, now that she had won.

"So am I," replied Jessica, politely, distantly.

"I shall say nothing of this interview to Linton."

"No."

Mrs. Romney rose to leave. She hesitated. "How will you tell him?" she asked.

"I won't have the courage to tell him," said Jessica, her voice very even and quiet and almost concealing the underlying note of bitterness. "I shall simply go away and leave him a letter."

Catherine Romney's face looked relieved. "That will be best," she agreed. She hesitated for another moment, then turned and walked quickly out of the room. Jessica remained seated for perhaps ten more minutes, and then she, too, rose and walked steadily out the door and down to the carriage that was to take her back to Montpelier Square.

# Chapter Nineteen

Love is a law, a discord of such force
  That twixt our sense and reason makes divorce.
—ANONYMOUS

They had dinner at home that evening. Linton had been out when Jessica returned to Montpelier Square and she had spent an hour lying quietly on her bed conducting a private and unpleasant inventory. Her conversation with Mrs. Romney had merely confirmed what she had known all along. She could not marry Linton. There was no path that pride, regard, convention, self-respect, and conscience did not block. Nor could she remain with him until March as she had originally planned. He would not wait that long for her answer. And she was afraid to lie and tell him she would marry him. She no longer trusted her ability to deceive him.

She would have to sell the necklace, she decided ruthlessly. That would more than pay for the interest she owed Mr. King. She would do it tomorrow, she thought, despair like dust in her throat. There was no point in prolonging this agony any longer.

Linton was in a carefree mood that evening. He had spent a few hours that afternoon discussing a Reform Bill with Mr. Grey and he was delighted at the thought of returning soon to Staplehurst. He told Jessica all about his home during dinner and she smiled and listened and encouraged him, all the while knowing in her heart she would never see it.

They went into the drawing room after dinner and she asked him a few more questions, the questions of someone curious about a place she is soon to visit. He was sitting in his favorite chair in front of the fire and she sat across from him, her eyes hungry on his strong, cleanly planed face, her ears drinking in the sound of his deep yet curiously soft voice. She watched the brilliant blue of his eyes, the laughter at the corner of his mouth. Philip, she said silently to herself, over and over. Philip.

The tea tray came in, and as she made the tea and handed him a cup the thought came to her that she would ask nothing more out of life than this, that she should sit just so every night and make him his tea. If she could only stop time and hold this moment forever, she thought. Silence had fallen, but it was the rich silence of deep, inarticulate companionship. He put down his cup and smiled at her, long and lazily. "Let's go to bed," he said.

She slept very little that night. She lay quietly against his hard body, and the pain within her was almost unendurable. One more day, she told herself. I will pay off the mortgage tomorrow and buy a ticket on the mail. The day after tomorrow I shall go.

Toward morning she fell asleep and so did not hear him when he got up. She woke as he came back, fully dressed, into the bedroom. "What time is it?" she asked.

He laughed at her. "Eight-thirty, sleepy one. I have an engagement to talk to a man about buying apples and I probably won't see you until after lunch."

"Why do you want to buy apples?" she asked, puzzlement and sleep clogging her voice.

He grinned. "I don't want to buy apples, I want to sell them. My agent has written me about this fellow, so I think I had better see him while I'm here in London." He crossed to the bed and leaned over, kissing her hard and fierce and quick. "I'll see you later," he murmured, his mouth still lightly touching hers. "And I'll want an answer."

"Yes." She watched as he walked away from her and out of the room, and lay back against her pillows once more, her eyes closed.

She transacted her business without difficulty. Mr. King was not happy to see his loan repaid so promptly. He would have liked to have gotten his hands on Winchcombe, but the interest he had made was ample and he was quite pleasant to Jessica.

Her encounter with Mr. King had been far more comfortable than an encounter she had had with Lord Alden earlier in the day. She had been coming out of Hoare's Bank just as Lord Alden was alighting from his phaeton.

"Miss O'Neill. What an unexpected pleasure." His strange greenish eyes had glinted between half-closed lids, and Jessica found herself repressing a slight shudder. There was something about this man that gave her a physical and moral chill.

"Lord Alden," she said, nodded curtly, and made to walk past him. He stepped in front of her.

"The theatre has sorely missed your presence," he said in his silky voice, and looked at her with eyes that undressed her.

Jessica felt her temper rising. "Indeed?" she replied coldly. "If you will excuse me, my lord, I must be going."

"Have you thought of my offer at all?" he asked.

"No."

His eyes narrowed even more until they were barely slits in his masklike face. "I see I have in Linton a formidable rival."

Jessica's eyes were gray ice. "There is not even a contest," she said, and pushed past him to walk to her waiting carriage.

She had arrived home in time for lunch. Linton came in about three o'clock and they decided to go for a ride in the park. When Jessica came downstairs dressed in her riding habit she found him in the hall holding a piece of notepaper in his hand. There was a slight frown between his golden brows, but his forehead smoothed as he looked up and saw her. "I'm afraid I'm going to have to bow out of our ride, Jess. I've just gotten a note from my mother. She is in town. I'll have to go and see her."

"Of course," she answered quietly.

He stood absorbed in thought for a moment and the frown crept back between his brows. "I'll be back tomorrow before lunch," he said then, decisively. "Don't look for me tonight."

"All right." Her voice gave no hint of the desolation that had just swept through her. She would not see him again.

He bent over and lightly kissed her cheek. "Chin up, darling," he murmured, then he left.

"Will you still be wanting your horse, Miss O'Neill?" the butler asked her.

"No. I mean, yes," she answered. After all, she had to do something to fill in the hours until tomorrow morning.

She did not sleep at all that night. The mail coach to Cheltenham was not leaving until eleven in the morning, and at six-thirty she rose, put on her riding habit, and walked around to the stables. She felt she had to get out of the house for a while. The hours of the night had been interminable.

Jerry, the groom who usually looked after her horse, was not around, so Jessica saddled the black mare herself. As she was leading Windswept out of the stable Francis, the young boy who assisted in the stable work, appeared with a bucket of water. Jessica smiled at him. "I am taking Windswept for a ride in the park. I shan't be gone more than an hour."

"Yes, ma'am," the boy said, and watched as she walked the horse out of the yard.

Twenty minutes later Jerry appeared. "Where's the mare?" he asked.

"The lady took him out," returned his subordinate.

Jerry swore with picturesque amplitude. "That

mare has a loose shoe," he explained as he saddled Linton's horse. "She came in with it yesterday. I'd better go after her or she's going to have to walk home." He finished saddling Linton's bay stallion, vaulted into the saddle, and clattered out of the stableyard. He was a block from Hyde Park when he saw Jessica coming out through the gate leading Windswept. "I knew it," he muttered to himself and prepared to urge the bay into a canter when he saw a carriage stop in front of Jessica. He pulled up for a minute, and as he watched a dark-haired man in evening dress got out. He turned to say something to the groom who rode beside the driver on the box, and the man jumped down and went to take the horse from Jessica. She appeared to be arguing with the man and Jerry again began to walk the bay down the street toward her. Then, with a suddenness that stunned him, the tall man opened the coach door, grabbed Jessica ruthlessly, and thrust her inside. She screamed once; then the coach door closed and drove briskly off.

Jerry pulled the bay stallion up once more. The groom holding Jessica's horse began to walk it slowly away, and Jerry looked carefully at his livery, memorizing the colors and markings. Then he turned the bay and rode as fast as he could through the London streets to Grosvenor Square.

Linton's meeting with his mother had not been comfortable for Lady Linton. She had spoken the truth when she had told Maria that she never interfered in her son's affairs. But there were times, she had thought to herself as she waited in the Grosvenor

Square house for Linton to present himself, when one was justified in interfering. If the circumstances were such that a loved one's actions were sure to be ruinous, then coercion from the outside was needed. And she was here to apply that coercion.

They had passed the afternoon pleasantly enough. It was after dinner, as they sat in the drawing room before a warm fire, that Lady Linton introduced the subject that had brought her to London. "When are you coming home to Staplehurst, Philip?" she asked.

His long fingers were laced together, and he regarded her over them thoughtfully. "Very soon now, mother. And I shall be bringing my wife home with me."

"So it is true," his mother said slowly. "You are serious about this Jessica O'Neill."

"Yes."

Lady Linton looked at the shining blond head of her beloved son and then into the brilliant blue of his eyes. She recognized the look his face wore. Under so much that was gentle, patient, and civilized Linton had passions that were fiercely strong and tenacious. When he gave his love and his loyalty he did not change. If he really loved this girl . . . "What do you know about this Jessica O'Neill, Philip?" she asked quietly. "What is her family? I did not think I would ever have to remind you of this but you have a duty to your own family, to your name and to the ancient rank you carry. An Earl of Linton may not do as he pleases, as may another man."

A gleam had come into those very blue eyes of his. "No, mother, you do not have to remind me of who I am." His voice was kept, with perceptible effort, quiet and ordinary. "Miss O'Neill is a woman that even an Earl of Linton would be proud to call his wife."

"So you think, my son. There are others who will think differently."

"If you are one of those others I shall be sorry, mother," he replied steadily.

She leaned forward, pleadingly, in her chair. "Philip, think about what you are doing. Please."

"I have thought about it," he returned. "My mind is made up."

They had separated for the night not long after that. Linton had not slept well in his solitary bed, and when a footman came into him at a little after seven-thirty he was wide awake. "My lord," the servant said hesitatingly, relieved at least not to be waking him. "There is a groom here from Montpelier Square. He insists he must see you immediately. He says it is an emergency."

Linton threw back his covers. "Show him up." When Jerry entered the vast bedroom a few minutes later he found the Earl of Linton with his hair tousled and wearing a dressing gown. "What has happened?" Linton asked curtly.

Jerry told him what he had seen. He described the servant's livery. Linton swore. "Alden!" he said grimly. "He lives in Mount Street. I'll go at once." His eyes, filled with a cold blue light, briefly rested on his groom's face. "Thank you. You were right to come to me." He nodded, and Jerry backed hastily out of the room. He was glad he wasn't the one who was going

158

to have to face the Earl when he had that look in his eyes.

It took Linton fifteen minutes to get to Mount Street. He left his groom holding the reins of his phaeton and ran up the steps of Alden's house. He tried the door and, surprisingly, found it open. He entered and made a swift search of the downstairs rooms. There was no one around. He took the steps two at a time, and at the sound of a man's voice he halted outside an upstairs door. Then Jessica spoke.

Linton tried the door, and this one was locked. "Open up, Alden," he said clearly, "or I'll shoot the lock off."

He heard Jessica cry, "Philip!" and then the door opened. She was standing at the far side of the room. Her hair had loosened and was falling on her shoulders. Her lip was cut; he could see blood on it. And she held a poker in her hand. A slow white rage took possession of Linton.

"Are you all right?" he asked her.

"Yes." She put down the poker and ran across the room to him. "Thank God you came, though."

"One of the grooms saw the incident." He turned from her to look at the man standing midway across the room. Alden took two steps back as he met that gaze.

"I didn't touch her, Linton," he said. "There's no need to look so grim."

"Go downstairs and wait for me," Linton said to Jessica.

She hesitated, looked at his face, and went. She walked halfway down the stairs then stopped. She had never seen Linton look like that. Suddenly she was afraid, even more afraid than she had been earlier. What was Philip going to do? She began to run back up the stairs. When she was nearly at the top her foot caught in the carelessly held-up length of her riding skirt. She felt herself losing her balance and grabbed for the rail. She missed and cried out as she toppled slowly, helplessly, down the long, elegant staircase.

The next thing she knew was Linton's face, bent over hers. From a long distance away she could hear his voice. He was calling her name. She made a great effort. "Yes?"

"Are you all right, Jess?" His face had come into focus for her now. He looked frightened. "Can you move?"

Slowly she tried to sit up. "Yes," she said again. She moved her legs. Her body was aching all over and her head hurt, but she could move. He bent and lifted her in strong arms and, gratefully, she rested her face against his shoulder. "My friends will call on yours, Alden," she heard him say, and then he strode out the front door, still holding her tightly in his arms.

# Chapter Twenty

If I could shut the gate against my thoughts
  And keep out sorrow from this room within
Or memory could cancel all the notes
  Of my misdeeds, and I unthink my sin.
                              —ANONYMOUS

As soon as they reached Montpelier Square Linton sent for the doctor. Dr. Bayer's diagnosis was that Jessica was painfully bruised and might have a slight concussion, but he didn't think any permanent damage had been done. He prescribed some medicine which caused Jessica to fall asleep almost immediately. She slept all through the day and did not awaken until eleven the following morning.

By then Linton had put a bullet through the Marquis of Alden's shoulder.

Lord George Litcham had tried to dissuade Linton from calling Alden out, but his words had fallen on deaf ears. "If you won't act for me, I'll get someone who will," said Linton relentlessly.

So Lord George had made the arrangements, and at six o'clock in the morning Linton and Alden had met out at Paddington and Linton had relieved his feelings by shooting Alden neatly through his right shoulder. Lord George had been enormously relieved. He had been afraid Linton had meant to kill Alden.

At two o'clock in the afternoon, as Linton was sitting on Jessica's bed watching her try to eat some soup, Lord George was presenting himself in Grosvenor Square. Lady Linton had heard about the duel.

Lord George started by pleading ignorance, but the look in Lady Linton's sapient blue eyes soon put him to rout. It wasn't long before he was telling her the whole story. It took a stronger man than Lord George to hold out against the combined charm and concern of Linton's mother.

"Evidently Alden was coming home after a night on the town," Lord George told her. "I doubt if he was sober. Well, stands to reason—how could he have been? Well, as he was driving by the park out came Miss O'Neill leading her horse. Alden stopped the carriage and got out. I imagine it looked like a perfect opportunity to him. From what he said I gather she had refused several offers from him; and not in a manner calculated to flatter him. He was after a little revenge it seems." Here Lord George recruited himself with a sip of sherry. Lady Linton said nothing. She just sat still and waited.

"So he pushed her into his carriage and forced her into his house. She evidently delayed him for some time by pretending to reconsider his offer. Then, when matters got serious, she grabbed the poker. That was when Linton arrived."

"I see."

"I have never seen Philip that angry. Never. There was no talking to him. I'm only glad he settled for Alden's shoulder."

"I'm glad it wasn't Philip who got shot," said Lady Linton tartly.

"Oh, there was never any fear of that," returned Lord George. "Linton is deadly with the pistols. You should have seen Alden's face. He was sick as a horse at having to face Philip. Of course there was nothing else he could do."

"Men!" said Lady Linton with scornful contempt. "As if a duel could ever solve anything. What does Miss O'Neill think of all this?"

"I doubt if she knows. You see she fell down the stairs at Alden's house and knocked herself out. The doctor gave her a sleeping draught and she was still sleeping this morning. Philip went right back to Montpelier Square after the meeting but I doubt if he'll tell her about it. I'm quite sure she wouldn't like it."

"She fell down the stairs? Is she hurt?"

"Not badly, thank God. If she had been seriously injured I really think Linton would have killed Alden."

"Well, I suppose we must be grateful for small blessings," snapped Lady Linton and dismissed the uncomfortable Lord George.

When Jessica awoke the next morning she felt achy and heavyheaded, which she put down to the aftereffects of Dr. Bayer's sleeping draught. The doctor came to see her again at about noon and recommended that she spend the rest of the day in bed. She alarmed Linton by submitting to the doctor's edict with scarcely a murmur.

By late afternoon she felt hot and ill, and when Linton felt her forehead it was cold with sweat. Once more he sent for the doctor. He was deathly afraid she had seriously injured her head in the fall, and when the doctor came slowly into the downstairs salon after seeing Jessica, Linton asked him sharply, "Is it brain fever?"

Dr. Bayer looked surprised. "No, my lord. It has nothing to do with her head. Indeed, if I had known about Miss O'Neill's condition I would have warned you this might happen. That was a very nasty fall she took."

"Her condition?" said Linton.

The doctor glanced at his face and then quickly looked away. "Miss O'Neill is three months pregnant. She is having a miscarriage."

"Will she be all right?" the Earl asked at last, his voice unusually harsh.

"Yes. It should be over soon, my lord. I'll stay with her."

"Is there anything you can do?"

"To save the child? No, my lord," the doctor's voice was firm but gentle. "She asked me the same thing. There is nothing to be done now, I'm afraid."

"I see."

The doctor returned upstairs, and about an hour

and a half later one of the servants came to tell Linton he could come upstairs if he wanted to.

The initial shock of the doctor's revelation to Linton had given way to a deep, quiet fury. He bitterly regretted his duel of that morning. He wished passionately that he had known then what he knew now. "I would have killed the bastard," he grated between clenched teeth. As he walked up the stairs to Jessica's room he felt that his limbs and movements were rigid with the anger that possessed him. He stopped outside her door for a minute to school his features; then he went in.

Jessica was lying quietly in bed; the doctor was standing by the window. The room was immaculate; there was no sign of what had just happened. Her head turned at the sound of the door opening. She saw him and her eyes suddenly came to life in the tired gray mask of her face. He stood still in the doorway for a long moment, his eyes on that face. He felt a wrench at his heart, so painful he could swear it was physical. Then everything inside him broke up, broke down and gave way, and he was sitting on the side of the bed holding her in his arms, his face buried in her hair. She began to cry, deep, hard sobs, and he held her closer, giving her the only comfort he could, the knowledge of his own grief and love.

Dr. Bayer ordered Jessica to stay in bed for four days, and she obeyed. She felt drained and empty, incapable of a thought that projected beyond the next hour. She had lost her baby. She could not bear to contemplate yet the loss of her love.

Linton was infinitely gentle with her. The blind fury that he had lived with since first he heard of her kidnapping had left him. He could not help Jessica by his anger. He had realized that as soon as he had seen her face. And she needed him. The fierce protectiveness that she had always aroused in him was his main emotion at present. It was why he asked her no questions, talked only of trivial, unemotional topics, and most of all gave her the steady comfort of his undemanding physical presence.

Lady Linton had not seen her son since he had left the house to rescue Jessica. He had written her a brief note telling her about Jessica's miscarriage. She had known he would have been happy had she come to Montpelier Square, but, holding fast to the news she had had from Mrs. Romney, the Countess had kept herself aloof. It seemed as if Linton's family did not need to save him from Jessica O'Neill, as the girl was prepared to do that herself. Lady Romney felt a pang of pity for Jessica, who obviously did love her son, but she did not want to do anything that might cause the actress to change her mind. If she thought Linton's mother would countenance such a marriage she might very well change her mind. So Lady Linton stayed away.

Her absence was not unnoticed by either Jessica or Linton, although it was unremarked upon. Linton was sorry. He did not want to cause a breach with his mother, but if she would not accept Jessica then a breach there would be.

Lady Linton's absence was far more bitter to Jessica. The Countess's judgment had been correct. Had she appeared in Montpelier Square Jessica would have weakened and allowed Linton to persuade her to agree to what her heart so sorely wanted. But his mother's absence said loudly that she was not prepared to accept such a marriage, and Jessica, as the days went by, was forced to realize that nothing had changed.

She had left home six months ago, and in that half-year's time her whole life had altered. She thought back now to the arrogant, innocent girl she had been. Not for her the sitting back and allowing destiny to take its course. Not for her a convenient marriage to some unknown, boorish, rich man. It was all right for other, less proud, less determined women. Not for her. Not for Jessica Andover.

She would take her fate into her own hands. She would dare to do what few women of her class would do. She would dare to stand alone.

She thought now she would have been wiser to marry Sir Henry Belton. He, at least, would never have been able to touch her. It might not have been a happy life, but there would not have been the soul-deep loneliness she knew was in her future now. It would be so hard to go on without him.

A week after the miscarriage she told Linton she wanted the carriage to go shopping. He was delighted. It was the first sign she had shown of coming out of the fog of depression that had gripped her all week. "Buy yourself some wedding clothes," he told her.

"We'll be married next week and go down to Staplehurst after."

She didn't go shopping at all. She bought a ticket for the next day's mail to Cheltenham.

# Chapter Twenty-One

Philip, the cause of all this woe, my life's content,
farewell!
—FULKE GREVILLE

It was just one more sleepless night out of a host of others, this, the last night she would lie beside him in the dark. She listened to his quiet, even breathing and thought how his nearness only made the pain the sharper. She was lying perfectly still, but quite suddenly she heard his voice. "Are you awake, Jess?" She moved her head a little, unable to speak, and then she was in his arms. "Don't grieve so, my darling," he said softly. "We must begin to think of the future now."

It was precisely the thought of the future that was causing her grief, but she couldn't tell him that. She clung to him. "Hold me, Philip. Love me."

His lips were against her temple. "I'm afraid I'll hurt you."

"I need you," she said in a strangled whisper.

"Jess . . ." His mouth came down over hers and his hands were gentle upon her and for the moment the loneliness receded as she gave herself to his growing passion. "Am I hurting you?" he asked.

She shook her head, and her voice was deep and

husky when she answered, "I love it when you come into me like this."

"God . . ." The careful restrictions he had been imposing on himself fell at her words, and they moved together with the urgency and hunger of a desperate need. When at last they lay quietly, satisfied and peaceful, she raised her hand and ran it lightly through his hair.

"I wanted a little boy with corn-colored hair and bright blue eyes," she said.

His body was still half covering hers and he smiled now and rubbed his rough cheek against her smooth one. "You'll have him," he promised. "And I'll have my red-headed little girl. We have years ahead of us to make a whole army of children."

She answered the only part of his speech that she could. "I don't have red hair."

He laughed. "Go to sleep, Jess." He turned her on her side and pulled her into the curve of his own body and she slept.

He wasn't there when she awoke, for which she was profoundly grateful. She had a cup of coffee, got dressed, and sat down to write him a letter. Then she ordered the carriage and had it take her to Madame Elliott's on Bond Street. She told the coachman to come back for her in two hours; as soon as he had driven off, she got into a hackney cab. Forty minutes later she was in the mail coach on her way to Cheltenham.

\* \* \*

Linton arrived back in Montpelier Square at about three in the afternoon. He had a special marriage license in his pocket and was eager to show it to Jessica. "My lord," Peter said to him as he let him into the house, "Miss O'Neill went out at ten this morning to drive to Bond Street. She has not yet returned."

Linton frowned at the man's grave face. "Well, she must have decided to go somewhere else afterward."

"No, my lord. Or at least she didn't go in the carriage. She told Jerry to return for her in two hours and when he did she wasn't there. What's more, they said at the dressmaker's that she had only stayed five minutes. She said she had a headache, and they got a hackney for her. But she didn't come back here."

Linton's eyes had begun to burn with a cold blue light as Peter told his story, but when he got to the part about the hackney Linton frowned. It couldn't have been Alden again, not if Jess had gone off voluntarily in a hackney. Besides, Alden was laid up with an injured shoulder. At this point Jessica's maid appeared in the hall.

"Miss O'Neill left a letter for you, my lord," she said somewhat breathlessly. "She asked me to give it to you when you came in."

Linton looked for a minute at the white envelope in the girl's hand, and a dreadful foreboding began to fill him. Very slowly he put up his hand, and when he had the envelope he walked into the drawing room and shut the door. He went to the window and stood there in the harsh light, his face white and strained.

With sudden decision he ripped open the envelope and took out the letter. Jessica's small, neat writing filled the page. With a taut line between his eyes he bent his head and read.

Montpelier Square, Wednesday
Dear Philip,

It is difficult, now that I have sat down to write this letter, to find the words to tell you all that is in my heart.

I love you. I shall never love anyone but you. And that is why I have left.

I find, after all, that I can write what I could not say to you. I cannot be your wife. I am not fit to be the wife of the Earl of Linton. I should injure you and disgrace you and that I cannot bear to do.

I could not say this to you because I know you would not allow me to. You would say you think me fit to be the wife of the best man in the world. But, my darling, others would think differently. And those others are ones so closely concerned with you, and would be so closely concerned with me, as to trouble the very foundation of our life together. I will not subject you to the sorrow of choosing between your wife and your family and friends.

You are not to worry about me. I have gone home to my family, where I am loved and needed. I shall be in no want. Except, of course, the want of you.

Forgive me. I wish I could say forget me, but I am not after all as selfless as that.

Jess

Linton finished reading the letter. He stared, unseeing, for a few moments longer at the neat lines of black script. He remembered last night. Then he closed his eyes. This was the thing he had feared the most, and it had happened. And he didn't even know where to begin to look for her. His eyes were a dark, bitter blue as he went upstairs and prepared to take apart all of her belongings in hopes of finding a clue to her real identity.

Jessica received a royal welcome home from Miss Burnley. The little governess had been frantic with worry over Jessica's sojourn in Scotland and when Jessica walked in the door of Winchcombe looking thin and tired but demonstrably alive Miss Burnley had wept with relief.

"I'm so glad to see you, my dear," she said for perhaps the fifteenth time as they sat in the morning parlor having tea. "It was such an anxious time. I always wondered if the letters we sent to that postal address you gave us in London ever reached you."

"Now Burnie, you know they did," Jessica said placatingly. "I always wrote back. But it was a very strange experience and not one I would care to repeat." Jessica's eyes closed briefly.

"I don't blame you," Miss Burnley said warmly, and bent forward to pat Jessica's hand. "It must have been dreadful, taking care of an old and dying woman."

"I think, if you don't mind Burnie, I'd rather not talk about it. Ever."

"All right, my dear. I understand." There was a pause; then the governess said tentatively, "Were you able to pay back Mr. King?"

"Yes." For the first time since she had come home Jessica smiled. "We're in the clear, Burnie. Winchcombe belongs to no one but me. We all of us, you and I and Geoff and Adrian, have a home that no one can take away from us."

"Thank God," said Miss Burnley devoutly.

"Thank Cousin Jean," Jessica said with pious hypocrisy.

She made the same comment two days later to Mr. Grassington. The lawyer had been strongly opposed to her borrowing money from a London moneylender but, as she had pointed out gently, she was of age and there was nothing he could do about it. He had acted as Jessica's intermediary and redeemed the Winchcombe mortgage from Sir Henry Belton. And he had always been skeptical about the sudden call from Cousin Jean Cameron.

"I don't believe a word of this story, Jessica," he told her now with a melancholy sigh. "I have no idea where you got that money, but it did not come from this mythical cousin. You may fool Miss Burnley and your brothers with that story but you cannot fool me."

Jessica shrugged, a small gesture that emphasized the thinness of her shoulders. "I am sorry you feel that way, Mr. Grassington."

"I have been worried to death about you," the old man said dispassionately.

"There was no need to worry. I am perfectly fine, as you can see for yourself. And Winchcombe is clear."

"You don't mean to tell me how you got that money?"

"You have heard the only explanation I am prepared to give."

He looked at her in silence for a tense moment. Then he nodded. "I think perhaps I do not want to know," he said a trifle grimly. He folded his hands on his desk. "The rest of your affairs are in order. If there is anything I can do for you please let me know."

Jessica's gray eyes softened. "You are always so good to me." She bent and kissed him on the cheek. "Come and dine with us next week."

"Thank you, my dear," he replied as he carefully polished his glasses. "I should like that very much."

# Chapter Twenty-Two

But I, who daily craving
Cannot have to content me,
Have more cause to lament me,
    Since wanting is more woe than too much
        having.
                                    —SIR PHILIP SIDNEY

News reached England at the beginning of March that Napoleon Bonaparte had escaped from Elba and landed in France. This great event effectively drew all the ton's interest from the affair of Philip Romney and Jessica O'Neill. Linton's duel with Lord Alden, Jessica's disappearance, and Linton's subsequently icy demeanor had all been a source of endless comment, but now the affairs of the world once again took precedence. London waited to hear that France had risen to halt Napoleon's march toward Paris. It learned instead that the Seventh Regiment had gone over to the Emperor at Grenoble and shortly after that the King's troops spontaneously changed sides, deserting the Bourbon King Louis XVIII. On March 20 Napoleon triumphantly entered the Tuileries.

Linton returned to Staplehurst at the end of March, and Lady Maria drove over from Selsey Place one afternoon to see him. "It will be war, Maria," he told her. "Have you heard from Matt?"

"He wrote to say that the Congress has declared Napoleon an outlaw. He says there will be war over Belgium if over nothing else. He thinks the alliance against Napoleon will reform."

"It already has. Wellington has been appointed commander-in-chief. You cannot possibly think of going to Vienna at this point."

"So Matt says too," replied Lady Maria reluctantly. "What a detestable little man Napoleon is. One had so hoped this dreadful war was over with for good."

"I know. Now there will be more bloodshed. And Castlereagh has pledged five million pounds sterling to the Allied army. That is bad news for the economy. Unfortunately there is nothing else to do but fight. Matt is right. Napoleon will never be satisfied until Belgium is part of France, and Britain can't and won't stand for that."

Lady Linton had come into the morning parlor shortly after that and Linton had excused himself to go and look at his new plantations. "I don't like the way Philip looks at all," his sister said immediately after he had gone.

"He has been like this for almost a month now," Lady Linton replied. "I am hoping that being here at Staplehurst will help. London was too hectic, too filled with memories. Now he is home he can busy himself with the things he loves. In time he will forget."

"She just walked out, mother?" Lady Maria asked. "Has he tried to find her? You wrote that she disappeared. It seems odd for a person of such celebrity to be able to do that."

"Evidently her name was not really O'Neill and the history she gave to the Covent Garden management was fictitious. No one knows who she really is. I will say that I am convinced she loved Philip." There was a pause, and Lady Linton raised sober eyes to her daughter's. "I saw the letter she left him."

"Oh?" Maria's brows were raised.

"Yes. Catherine Romney had talked to her; I wrote you that. Evidently Catherine made a very strong impression on the girl. She wrote Philip that she was not fit to be the wife of the Earl of Linton."

Maria sighed. "It is a thousand pities that this had to happen. But she is right. Such a marriage would be impossible."

"I know, my dear. But it is breaking my heart to look at Philip."

The days went by. Linton resumed his old schedule of work at Staplehurst and followed the war news in the newspapers. On the surface, to his tenants and to his workmen, he seemed the same. But his mother saw the shadow of strain in his eyes, the grim, painful set of his mouth. All the lazy sunshine was gone from him. He was always pleasant, always courteous. But he was too often silent, and it was a silence whose quality made Lady Linton very uneasy.

May came, and June, and the armies of the coalition were assembling in Belgium. Sir Matthew Selsey was still in Vienna. He had written to his wife that she was to remain in England until he was able to join her sometime during the summer. Consequently Matthew and Lawrence Selsey, who were to have stayed at Staplehurst for the summer vacation if their mother was in Vienna, would be going instead to Selsey Place. Lady Linton didn't know whether to be glad or sorry. She thought perhaps his young nephews would have livened Linton up, if they didn't drive him distracted, which was the other possibility.

On June 19 word came to Staplehurst that Wellington had engaged Napoleon at Quatre Bras. Linton prepared to go up to London to await further news. His mother came into the library as he was writing out some instructions, and she stopped for a moment just inside the door and looked at his intent face. The sunlight from the window fell on the still, golden wing of his hair, the same thick silky gold that had clung to her fingers when she had brushed it in childhood. The clean angle of cheek and jawbone had long since lost all traces of childish softness, but she longed now to press her own cheek against his and comfort him as she had done so often long ago. He looked up. "Oh, there you are, mother. I am leaving to go up to London immediately. As soon as I know what has happened I'll return to tell you."

"All right, Philip," she answered steadily. "I think I shall ask Maria to come over. She will want to know the news as soon as possible, I'm sure."

"Very well." He had risen at her entrance, and he came across the room now to stand next to her. He was so tall, Lady Linton thought. "It seems a long time ago that I had to bend over to kiss you," she murmured as his lips brushed her cheek. He smiled but did not reply, and in a moment he was gone.

Late in the afternoon of June 22 the Earl of Linton stood in the window of Brooks'. Behind him young Lord Melville was telling a spellbound group of men that he knew for a fact that the Prussians had been wiped out, that the Anglo-Allied army had been destroyed and Wellington himself killed. In the middle of Melville's discourse Linton turned, touched him on the arm, and said, "Look there." Everyone immediately came to the window and, looking out, saw a chaise and four horses driving down the street followed by a running, cheering mob.

"What is that sticking out the windows?" asked Lord George Litcham.

Linton's eyes were very blue. "Those, George," he answered quietly, "are three French Imperial Eagles."

Shortly after that the tower guns began to fire a 101-gun salute, and church bells pealed out all over London. Once more Napoleon Bonaparte had been defeated.

"Well, I thank God we won but my heart goes out to the families of those who were slain," Lady Linton said as she, Maria, and Maria's two eldest sons sat listening to Linton's report on the morning of June 23.

"I know." Lady Maria's face was unusually serious as she replied to her mother's comment.

"I wish *I* had been there!" said Matthew Selsey enthusiastically.

"Well, I am very glad you were not," snapped his

mother instantly. "And let me tell you, young man, you have a great deal of growing up to do before you can even contemplate assuming such an adult role in the world. You've been sulking like a baby ever since you came home from school."

"I have not been sulking," said Matthew, a definite pout on his handsome, fair-skinned face.

"What has happened, Matthew, to cause you to be unhappy?" his grandmother asked gently.

"He thought he was going on a visit to Geoffrey Lissett," said Lawrence helpfully. "But it's been cancelled and Matt is mad as a hornet."

"If I had wanted you to answer my question, Lawrence, I would have asked you," Lady Linton said austerely.

Linton looked at his eldest nephew's flushed cheeks and said sympathetically, "Oh yes, I remember you mentioned the visit to me when I drove you back to Eton after Christmas. What happened, Matthew?"

"I don't know, Uncle Philip," the boy answered unhappily. "We had it all fixed up, Geoff and I. They have a stud and I was going to help with the horses. Mama said I might. She said it would keep me out of your hair for the summer."

Linton looked slightly amused. "Oh, did she?"

"I said you might go, Matthew, provided I heard from Geoffrey's sister that it was all right with her."

"And it wasn't all right, I gather?" Lady Linton inquired.

"No." Matthew's lip was definitely drooping. "I can't understand why she doesn't want me. I'd be a *help,* not a bother."

"Well, I can understand," his mother said briskly. "The poor girl is probably at her wit's end. I knew Geoffrey's father. Sir Thomas Lissett was a charming man who hadn't a notion of what the word self-discipline meant. There were rumors all over London that he was badly dipped. All of his debts probably landed in the lap of Geoffrey's sister. I have no doubt that that is why she is starting a stud."

"I know they need money. Geoff says he is *determined* to help put Winchcombe on its feet again. I know they could use extra help, and I'm good around horses, aren't I, Uncle Philip?"

Linton was looking at his nephew with a strange light in his eyes. "Tell me about the Lissetts, Matthew. How many of them are there? How old is Geoffrey's sister?"

"Oh, Philip," Lady Linton murmured despairingly, but he shook his head at her impatiently.

"Well, actually, Jess is only Geoffrey's half-sister," Matthew responded. He continued readily, unaware of the electric shock that his casual use of Jessica's name had produced in his elders. "She is the real owner of Winchcombe; it belonged to her father, not to Geoffrey's. There are just the two of them and Adrian, Geoff's younger brother. He's at Eton, too. What was the other thing you wanted to know, Uncle Philip?"

"What did you say Geoffrey's sister's name was?" Linton's voice, even to himself, was unrecognizable.

"Jessica. Her last name is Andover." There was a puzzled look in Matthew's eyes as he stared at his uncle.

"And where is this Winchcombe?"

"Just outside of Cheltenham."

Linton's eyes were brilliant. "Have you ever met Jessica, Matthew?"

"No, Uncle Philip."

"About how old is she?"

"Twenty-one or two, I think."

"Good heavens, Philip, surely you don't think. . . ?" It was his sister's voice, and he turned to look at her.

"I don't know what to think, Maria. I do know that I am leaving immediately for Cheltenham."

"Where is Uncle Philip going, mother?" Geoffrey asked as the door closed behind Linton. "To Winchcombe? Why? I don't understand."

His mother ignored him. Her magnificent green eyes were fixed on Lady Linton. "Is it possible?" she asked.

"I don't know, Maria," her mother answered. "But I find myself hoping very much that it is."

# Chapter Twenty-Three

Alas, my love! ye do me wrong,
    To cast me off discourteously;
And I have loved you so long,
    Delighting in your company.
              —ANONYMOUS

Ever since Jessica had returned to Winchcombe she had buried herself in work. Miss Burnley expostulated with her often but Jessica would not listen. The best way to manage the pain, she found, was to work herself to the point of exhaustion. Then, at least, she could sleep at night.

It was better when the boys came home from school, although she had had a moment of panic when she realized that Geoffrey wanted to invite Linton's nephew to spend the summer at Winchcombe. She had been tarter and more abrupt with Geoffrey than she had ever been before, and he had written to Matthew Selsey to cancel the invitation with very little protest. Both Geoffrey and Adrian were aware of a change in Jessica. She didn't seem to hear half of what was said to her, and she seldom laughed. Miss Burnley told them that Jessica was having a reaction to her experience in Scotland and that they must all be considerate and sensitive to her feelings. The boys tried, but they sorely missed their vibrant, intensely alive sister. This Jessica acted like a sleepwalker. The boys found themselves trying to keep as much out of her way as possible.

Geoffrey and Adrian were coming down the front steps of Winchcombe after lunch on the afternoon of June 24 when a smart phaeton drawn by a pair of matched grays came trotting up the driveway. Both boys stayed at the bottom of the steps, their eyes fixed admiringly on the horses. The phaeton was drawn up before them and a man asked in a deep, quiet voice if this was Winchcombe.

"Yes, it is," replied Adrian.

"I say, sir, that is a bang-up pair of grays!" said Geoffrey enthusiastically.

"Thank you," Linton responded courteously. "You must be Geoffrey Lissett. I should like very much to see your sister if she is at home."

"She went into Cheltenham this morning to see Mr. Grassington, our lawyer. But she should be back soon. Should you like to wait for her, sir?"

"Yes," said Linton decisively. "I should."

"If you like I'll drive your phaeton down to the stables and you can wait in the drawing room," Geoffrey said eagerly.

Linton had heard enough about Geoffrey Lissett's horsemanship to allow him to agree. A delighted Geoffrey, with Adrian beside him, climbed up into the driver's seat, and Linton ascended the front steps of Jessica's home.

Stover, the butler who had been at Winchcombe

**185**

since before Jessica was born, answered the door and showed him into the drawing room. He was looking around him at the peaceful harmony of faded ivory, crimson, pink, and blue that was Winchcombe's drawing room when the door opened and a small, brown-haired woman who was dressed simply but tastefully in a dress of French blue cambric entered. "Lord Linton?" she asked in a beautiful, clear voice.

He came toward her. "Yes, I am Linton. Your butler said I might wait here for Miss Andover to return."

"Of course," the small woman replied. "Please do sit down. I am Miss Burnley, Miss Andover's former governess. May I offer you some refreshment, Lord Linton?"

He was on the point of refusing when he changed his mind. "A glass of sherry, thank you."

The sherry was brought and served and Miss Burnley, who was obviously dying to know what his business was with Jessica, maintained a gallant flow of light conversation. "Did you meet Miss Andover while she was in Scotland?" she finally ventured.

He looked surprised. "No. I didn't realize she had been in Scotland."

"Yes. She was there for most of the winter. A cousin of her mother's was ill and Miss Andover went to look after her."

He looked thoughtful for a moment, and then he smiled at Miss Burnley. It was a smile Jessica knew well, the warm, lazy, genuinely sweet smile that undid almost everyone he turned it on. Miss Burnley melted in its radiance. "Did this cousin by any chance leave Jess some money?"

The smile, his title, his blond good looks, his use of Jessica's first name, all somehow reassured Miss Burnley that it was perfectly all right for her to confide in him. Afterwards, when she was reflecting soberly on the interview, she did not understand how she had been so forthcoming, but forthcoming she certainly was. "Yes," she said now in answer to his question. "Miss Cameron left her quite a lot of money. Enough, thank God, to pay off the mortgage on Winchcombe."

"I see. That was certainly fortunate."

"Yes. I must say I was very worried when Jessica borrowed the money from Mr. King to pay off Sir Henry. And I still cannot quite see why she found it so impossible to marry him. But, thank God, it all turned out for the best in the end."

Linton didn't answer right away, he was occupied with what Miss Burnley had told him. The little governess, looking at him, thought she had never in her life seen anyone with eyes so blue. "How is the stud going?" he asked then.

"Jessica seems to be pleased with it," returned Miss Burnley. "It is a tremendous amount of work, however. I have been begging her to take on more help but she says we can't afford it. Geoffrey is very helpful, of course, but he is in school for most of the year."

He started to answer her when there came through the opened window the sound of horses' hooves on the gravel. Clear as a bell on the summer air Jessica's voice floated to Linton's ears. "Take the horses down to the stables, Jem. I'll be down shortly myself. Tell Geoffrey to saddle up Northern Light."

Linton's heart was hammering. Until he had heard her voice he had not been sure. "Miss Burnley," he said urgently, "go out and ask Jess to come in here. Don't tell her who I am. Just say there is someone to see her. Please."

Miss Burnley hesitated, looked at his face, nodded, and left the room. Linton heard her voice in the hall saying, "There is someone to see you, my dear, in the drawing room. I think it is about one of the horses."

"Oh?" There was the sound of Jessica's swift, long steps as she came across the hall. She opened the door of the drawing room and stopped as abruptly as if she had walked into glass. Miss Burnley, behind her, almost bumped into her.

"Hello, Jess," he said steadily. "How are you?"

"What are you doing here? How did you find me?" Her voice sounded thin and strained. There was absolutely no color in her face.

"My nephew was very disappointed at not being allowed to come to Winchcombe. When he told me a little about your family I began to suspect. I came to find out for sure." There was a pause, then he said, the bitterness just audible under his deep, even tone, "You have put me through hell, do you know that?"

Her eyes, open and dark, were on his face. At his last words the color came flooding back to her cheeks. "I know. I'm sorry. You shouldn't have come."

"Well I have come," he replied crisply, "and you are damn well going to listen to me. Come in here and sit down."

"Jessica . . ." said Miss Burnley nervously, and they both jumped a little and turned to look at her. So absorbed had they been in each other that they had forgotten the governess's existence.

"It's all right, Burnie," Jessica said then.. "This is Lord Linton. I know him." She turned once more to look at the man behind her. Their eyes held for a full three seconds. Then Jessica turned back to Miss Burnley. "Leave us alone, Burnie. I am perfectly safe with Lord Linton."

Miss Burnley looked doubtfully at Linton, then at Jessica. She sighed a little but dutifully turned and left the room quietly, closing the door behind her. Jessica then crossed to a pale pink sofa and sat down abruptly, as if her legs wouldn't hold her any longer. "Why did you come?" she asked him. "You had my letter. Surely you must see the truth of what I wrote. Why stir up the pain again?"

He stood where he was, next to a polished rosewood table. "You look too thin," he said. "Miss Burnley says you are working too hard." He paused, debating how to begin, his eyes on her averted face. "Why wouldn't you marry Sir Henry, Jess?" he asked at last very softly.

Her head jerked around at his words. "What do you know about Sir Henry?"

"Very little. Just that you refused to marry him. I know also that you needed money. But then I always knew that."

She rubbed her forehead a little as if it were aching. "True. There was never much secret about that."

"No."

She smiled a little at his monosyllabic reply. "It's very simple, really," she told him. "Sir Henry Belton is a neighbor and the owner of Melford Hall. When my stepfather died he left a load of debt, and Sir Edmund Belton, who was Henry's uncle and a friend of my father's, agreed to hold a mortgage on Winchcombe. When Sir Edmund died his nephew Henry took over both Melford Hall and my mortgage. He told me if I didn't agree to marry him he would foreclose on Winchcombe." Her eyes were dark and enormous in her thin, narrow-boned face. "I would have lost it, Philip. I could not have allowed that to happen."

"So you decided to become a mistress rather than a wife."

Her lids dropped. "I don't expect you to understand."

"Every other woman in the world would have given in and married that bully," he said slowly. "But not you."

"I couldn't. I couldn't marry him. I knew what that meant, you see. I wouldn't have been myself, ever again. I couldn't do it. I didn't have the courage. I would have slept with him, but not marriage."

Her eyes had been on her hands, lying closed tightly together in her lap. She heard him say clearly, "Do you feel that way about marriage to me?"

She raised her eyes to his face and her mouth curled into something that was not quite a smile. "You know that I don't," she said softly.

"Then marry me."

"We have been through this, Philip. I cannot. There

are things which, if a woman does them, can never be forgotten."

"You are Jessica Andover. What you have done is of no moment."

"That is not true," she replied steadily.

"Are you afraid of exposure then?"

"I should not relish it, but that is not what is holding me back."

He tried another tack. "And am I to be punished, then, because of what you have done? Is that your sense of justice? If you tell me now that you do not love me I will go away and trouble you no more. But if you love me, after what has passed between us, I have a right to demand that you marry me. I do demand it." He came closer to where she sat on the sofa. "Tell me, Jess," he said imperiously, "tell me you don't love me."

The strain this interview was putting on her was evident in her too intense stillness. "It is not that I do not love you," she said at last. "Quite the contrary. It is just that you are out of my reach."

He ran his hand through his hair in frustration. He had never before come up against a force in her that he could not move. The day was very warm, and threads of gold, dislodged by his impatient fingers, spangled the dampness on his forehead. "Go away," she said, the line of her mouth thin and taut with pain. "Go away and forget me."

"I am no good hand at forgetting," he replied.

"Philip," she said. "Please."

His nostrils were pinched and there was a white line around his mouth. "If there is one thing in this world that I abhor," he said bitterly, "it is unnecessary sacrifice."

Her hands, still clasped in her lap, were white with pressure. "I did not think you could be so cruel." Her voice sounded as if she had lost her breath.

He made an involuntary gesture toward her, then checked himself. "I'll go, Jess. But I'll be back." He walked steadily to the door, opened it, and without a backward look exited from her presence. She watched him go in silence and the thought crossed her mind that his erect blond head had the look of a war helm. She had no doubt that he would be back.

# Chapter Twenty-Four

What fools are they that have not known
That love likes no laws but his own?
—FULKE GREVILLE

Linton drove straight through to Staplehurst. He arrived in the early morning hours when the house was asleep and went to his room to lie on his bed, sleepless until morning broke and he could see his mother.

Lady Linton always dressed and came downstairs to breakfast, and this morning she was extremely surprised to find her son waiting for her. "Philip! I had not expected you back so soon," she said. Then, looking at his tired, somber face, she asked hesitantly, "Was it she?"

"Yes."

Relief flooded through Lady Linton, but her emotion was not reflected in the stern face of her son. She seated herself across from him at the table. "Then what is the matter?" she asked gently.

He sat down again himself and his eyes, almost black with fatigue and unhappiness, fixed themselves on his mother's sympathetic face. "She won't have me, mother."

"Because of what Catherine Romney said to her? she said after a pause.

He frowned, his attention suddenly focused. "What is this about Catherine Romney?"

Too late Lady Linton realized her mistake. "Tell me, mother," he was saying, a very grim note in his voice, and Lady Linton sighed a little.

"Very well. After you asked her to marry you, your Jessica sought out Catherine. She wanted to know what your family and friends would think of such a match." Lady Linton shrugged a little. "Well, Philip, what was poor Catherine to say?"

"I gather then it was she who told Jess that I should be disgraced and dishonored if she married me."

"Yes."

Linton swore. Then he looked levelly into his mother's eyes. "And do you feel the same way, mother?"

"I did, Philip," she answered honestly. "I do not feel that way any longer."

His eyes began to get bluer. "Really, mother? Would you accept Jess if we married? Welcome her to Staplehurst?"

"Yes."

He drank some coffee, frowning a little in abstraction, his mind racing. "It seems to me," he heard his mother's voice saying calmly, "that if you are really going to marry this girl we had better make plans to assure that she will be received by society."

"I don't even know if she'll marry me, mother," he said tautly. "I am just hoping that your acceptance will make a difference to her."

"What will make a difference to her is the knowledge that marriage to her has not injured your

**194**

position with either your family or your friends. If you want her to agree to be your wife, you must reassure her on both those matters."

He was paying very close attention to her. "She is of good birth, mother. The Andovers have been at Winchcombe for centuries."

"I remember her father as a young man." Lady Linton folded her hands in her lap. "Philip, how did a girl like that ever decide to go on the stage and how did she ever agree to become your mistress?"

He told her. When he had finished, all she said slowly was, "I see."

"Under those circumstances, mother, can she be accepted by society? It doesn't matter a damn to me what anybody else thinks, but you are right in saying it does matter to Jess."

"The person you need to help you, my son, is Maria," Lady Linton said with decision.

"Maria?"

"Certainly. She is one of the patronesses of Almack's. There are very few women more powerful in the closed world of London society than your sister, my dear. If Maria agrees to sponsor Jessica, I think you may say that any objections society might have will crumble."

He was silent for a minute, assessing what she had said. "But will Maria agree to sponsor Jess? It is hardly the kind of marriage she has been trying to promote for me for years."

"I remember you once told me that if you were in trouble there is no one you would rather go to than

Maria." She raised her brows at him. "I think you are in trouble now, my son."

"I am," he replied soberly. "The worst trouble of my life."

"Well then?"

"I'll ride over to Selsey Place," he replied. He rose from the table and bent to kiss her before he left the room.

Maria was in the drawing room arranging in a vase the flowers she had just cut when her brother walked in. "Philip!" She pushed the last rose haphazardly into the middle of her careful arrangement and turned to him expectantly. "What happened? Is she your Jessica?"

He noted with a flicker of pleasure that both his mother and his sister had referred to Jess as "your Jessica." "Yes," he said. "She is."

"I can't believe it," Maria said, fixing wide eyes on him. "Jessica O'Neill is really Jessica Andover of Winchcombe. Imagine."

"Maria, sit down. I have to talk to you. I need your help."

She moved to a striped silk armchair and sat down. "Oh?" she said. "What is it I can do for you, Philip?"

He remained standing but leaned an arm on the mantelpiece. He took a deep breath and spoke in a carefully controlled voice. "I want to tell you first about Jess, about why she did what she did." Maria's green eyes brightened, and she nodded. Linton went on. "Part of it you know already. You said you knew Jess's stepfather, Lissett, and that you suspected he

196

had left her saddled with a mountain of debt." She nodded again. "You were right. To pay off the creditors she mortgaged Winchcombe. The friend of her father's who held the mortgage died and his nephew succeeded. The nephew told Jess that if she didn't marry him he would foreclose on her. Winchcombe was all she had left to support herself and her brothers. She couldn't lose it."

He paused and Maria said in a neutral tone, "Why wouldn't she marry this man, then?"

"It is hard to understand if you don't know Jess," he replied. "She is so proud, Maria, so independent. She said to me, 'I would never be myself again if I married him.'"

Maria's full lips compressed a little. "She also had first-hand knowledge of just how helpless a woman can be. Thomas Lissett probably milked Winchcombe for everything he could get out of it. It didn't belong to him; it belonged to Jessica, but because she was a minor he could do it. A married woman's property, unless careful steps are taken, is legally as under the control of her husband as a minor's property is under the control of a guardian."

"Yes. She knew that as well."

"And so she decided to get the money for the mortgage in the only way that is open to a woman other than marriage?"

"Yes."

"I don't think I would have had the courage," Maria said candidly.

He took his arm off the mantel and turned to face her fully. "Jess has more courage in her little finger

**197**

than most men I know have in their entire bodies. And I am not speaking just of physical courage but of a lonely, cold-blooded moral courage that very few possess." He spoke with a rough force that impressed Maria almost as much as his words did.

"What do you want me to do, Philip?" she asked.

He pulled up a chair and sat close beside her. "She won't marry me, Maria. Catherine Romney told her some nonsense about my being disgraced and dishonored by such a marriage and now she refuses to listen to reason. The only chance I have of changing her mind is to convince her that both my family and the society I move in will accept her as my wife. That is where I need your assistance."

"What did mother say?"

"Mother suggested that I ask you to sponsor Jess into society." There was a pause. "Will you, Maria?"

Maria was frowning thoughtfully, the thin arched lines of her brows drawn together, her forehead charmingly puckered. "If she had been a nobody from the backwaters of Ireland it would have been impossible. But she is an Andover . . ." Maria paused and Linton sat silent. "Her mother was a Frenchwoman if I remember correctly," Maria continued after a moment. "I vaguely remember meeting her many years ago. Nothing wrong with the family on that side either."

"There is nothing wrong with *her*," Linton said then, forcefully.

Maria's green eyes rested inscrutably on her brother's face, then she smiled. "I once told mother I wondered what kind of a girl it would take to make an impression on you. I must say I never envisioned this."

He responded more to her smile than to her words. "You'll do it?"

"I will."

He leaned over to kiss her cheek. "You are a paragon of sisters, Maria, and I hereby eat every word I may have said to the contrary." She laughed, and he continued, a note of anxiety creeping into his voice. "It can be done, you think?"

Maria drew herself up regally. "My dear Philip, if I choose to present a person as acceptable you may be sure she will be regarded as such by anyone at all who matters in London."

He grinned. "You are a trump, Maria. Now I have just got to convince Jess."

"That might not be so easy," Maria murmured. "I could convince her far more easily than you. She may think you are being overly optimistic."

"Maria." His hand closed over hers and the blue of his eyes was almost blinding. "Come with me to Winchcombe."

Her own eyes began to sparkle, then clouded with disappointment. "How can I? There's the baby. She's not weaned yet, Philip. I can't leave her."

He sat back. "Of course. How stupid of me. Well, perhaps you would send Jess a letter?"

Her eyes narrowed a little. "Would you mind travelling with a baby?" she asked.

"Of course I wouldn't mind! Do you think you might come?"

"If I do, I shall have to bring Elizabeth."

"Fine. Marvelous. Wonderful. Anything I can do for either of you, you have only to ask."

A very self-satisfied look descended on Maria's beautiful features. "I seem to recall you once told me not to help you any more," she said blandly.

"I must have been mad," he replied promptly.

"Philip, in order to see you in this state of grateful submission I would do anything," she declared with enormous pleasure. "When do we start?"

# Chapter Twenty-Five

Greensleeves, now farewell! adieu!
　God I pray to prosper thee;
For I am still thy lover true
　Come once again and love me.
　　　　　　　—ANONYMOUS

For the second time in a week Miss Burnley was surprised to find the Earl of Linton calling at Winchcombe. And this time he had his sister with him. Stover had shown Linton and Maria into the drawing room before he went to inform Miss Burnley of the visitors' arrival. For the moment Maria had left the baby in the carriage with her nurse. As she entered the room Miss Burnley was conscious of a feeling of distinct trepidation. She had gotten little out of Jessica about the Earl of Linton but it had been very clear that his visit had upset her badly. Miss Burnley was afraid that money trouble had risen to plague them once again.

"Miss Andover is down at the stables, my lord," she told Linton as she came into the room. "I have sent someone to inform her of your arrival."

Linton smiled at the small, obviously troubled woman. "Thank you, Miss Burnley. Allow me to introduce to you my sister, Lady Maria Selsey."

Maria smiled at Miss Burnley as well. "You are Miss Andover's old governess, are you not?" she asked.

"Yes, my lady."

Maria looked thoughtfully at Miss Burnley's anxious face. "I think we should take Miss Burnley into our confidence, Philip."

"If she doesn't already know my errand," Linton put in drily.

"No, my lord, I do not," replied Miss Burnley more crisply than usual.

"It is very simple, really," he said with a charming, rueful smile. "I want Miss Andover to marry me. She, although she says she loves me, refuses to do so. She insists she would not be accepted by my family. To prove to her that she is wrong I have brought my sister all the way from Kent to see her."

"I see," said Miss Burnley faintly. She did not see at all, of course. Where had Jessica met this man? And why should she feel unacceptable to his family? Miss Burnley looked with wide eyes at Lady Maria Selsey, whose fame had penetrated even to the Assembly Rooms of Cheltenham. That elegant lady said now, with crisp decision, "Philip, I think I should see Miss Andover by myself, so you will please go and wait in some other room until I send for you. Miss Burnley, I have my four-month-old daughter in the carriage. Would you mind showing my nurse to a spare bedroom where she can care for the baby until I am ready to leave?"

"Certainly, my lady," said a startled Miss Burnley.

She turned to Linton. "Should you care to wait in the library, Lord Linton?"

"That sounds fine, Miss Burnley," he replied, and the two of them moved to the door. Linton cast one more quick glance at his sister, then followed Miss Burnley out.

When Jessica was informed that the Earl of Linton had called, her first impulse was to refuse to see him. Further reflection had changed her mind. If she wouldn't go to him he was perfectly capable of seeking her out, and she did not want to meet him in the full view of her brothers. Obviously the only thing for her to do was to see him and to convince him that she had meant every word she said to him the other day.

"Where is he, Burnie?" she said tensely to a waiting Miss Burnley at the door of the house.

"Your visitor is in the drawing room, my dear," replied that lady with a scrupulous regard for accuracy.

Jessica said nothing else but walked swiftly across the hall, opened the door of the mentioned room, and once again stopped dead on the threshold. Inside was a very beautiful fair-haired woman who was dressed in a fashionable walking dress of almond green. The woman was looking at her appraisingly, and Jessica was suddenly conscious of her ancient riding skirt, open-necked shirt, and rolled-up sleeves. Brilliant color stained her cheeks and her chin elevated a quarter of an inch. "Yes?" she said in a cool voice. "May I help you?"

Maria heard the edge in that voice and realized she had offended. It was not, in fact, Jessica's clothes at which she had been staring but at Jessica herself. She had not known what to expect, but this tall, slender girl with her thin, proud face, direct gray eyes, and thick braid of brown hair falling almost to her waist satisfied Maria's imagination. She had not expected a conventional beauty. She smiled now, a more brilliant, less warm smile than her brother's, but still a smile calculated to disarm. "I beg your pardon for staring," she said, "but I have been most anxious to meet you. I am Maria Selsey, Philip's sister. He asked me to come to see you."

The high color drained from Jessica's face, leaving the pearly curve of the skin over her cheekbones looking thin and white. She said nothing. Maria regarded her with suddenly serious eyes. This interview was not going to be easy; the girl's face looked guarded and faintly hostile. Plainly Maria's smile had not made its proper impression. "May we sit down?" Maria said slowly. "I have travelled quite a long way and I have several things of importance to say to you."

Still in silence Jessica crossed the floor and sat, straight-backed, in a faded armchair six feet from Maria. Maria seated herself gracefully in the chair that stood behind her and regarded the young face across from her thoughtfully. "I have not come on Catherine Romney's errand, Jessica," she said at last, quite gently. Jessica's eyelids flickered but otherwise her expression did not change.

"Oh?" she said unencouragingly.

"No," Maria continued, speaking now with quiet emphasis. "I came to tell you that should you decide to marry Philip my mother will welcome you into the family and I will undertake to see to it that you are received by society as the Countess of Linton should be."

The sudden widening of Jessica's eyes betrayed her surprise. "I don't think I understand you," she said faintly.

"I did not think you would, which was why I came," Maria returned soberly. "You were told the opposite story rather brutally by Catherine Romney, I understand."

"Mrs. Romney was frank," replied Jessica a little stiffly. "I had no communication from any other member of your family."

Maria smiled a trifle ruefully. "I know. And I would not be truthful if I did not say that my mother and I did not regard with favor the idea of a marriage between you and my brother." Her smile became warmer, infectiously charming. "We have since changed our minds."

Jessica's head was in a whirl. She found it hard to comprehend that this was actually Philip's sister who was sitting here, smiling at her, speaking of welcoming her into the family! "And what was it that caused such a change?" she managed to say at last.

"Two things, actually. The first and the less important was our discovery of who you are. You must realize yourself that Jessica Andover of Winchcombe is a very different matter from Jessica O'Neill, Irish actress of unknown origin."

Jessica's eyes, wide and dark and unreadable, were fixed on Maria's face. "And the second?" she asked steadily.

"The second was Philip." Maria looked straight back into Jessica's eyes, her own sober and worried and earnest. "I love my brother," she said clearly. "I did not realize what losing you would do to him." For the first time Maria saw a change in the self-contained face of the girl she was addressing. "And it won't get any better," she continued. "Philip is not the kind who forgets."

Jessica made a small, involuntary gesture with her hand, which was quickly stilled. The pallor of her cheeks had flushed to warm ivory. Maria leaned forward. "He loves you, Jessica. It didn't matter to him who you were. If you love him in return I think you owe it to him to marry him." She paused, then asked deliberately, "*Do* you love him?"

There was something in Jessica's face that caused Maria to avert her eyes for a moment. "I love him," the girl replied simply. "That is precisely why I would *not* marry him."

"Well, it was very noble of you," Maria said briskly, steering away from the shoals of emotion looming at her feet. "Our intentions were noble as well. In fact, we have all been so busy saving Philip from you that we have neglected a very important point. We have, among us, made the poor boy perfectly miserable. The time has come to put matters right."

"Can we?" asked Jessica, a faint gleam of hope glimmering deep within her eyes.

"Certainly. Your birth is excellent. Your conduct, once it is seen in the proper light, will be understandable."

"Will it?" The clear gray eyes were steady on Maria's face. "Do *you* understand it? Does Philip?"

"Philip's exact words to me were that you had more courage in your little finger than most men he knew had in their entire bodies." The gray eyes began to glow a little, and Maria continued, "I find I agree with him, Jessica." She folded her hands in her lap. "There will be a great deal of talk, of course. But if you are married in the presence of both our families and are introduced to society by my mother at a ball given by me, there is no one who will refuse to accept you."

The glow in Jessica's eyes was more pronounced. "Can that possibly be true?" she breathed.

Maria raised a haughty eyebrow. "Scandals worse than yours have been forgiven. Look at the Stanfords. Two years ago no one could talk of anything else. Today they are entrenched at the top of the ton. It all depends on how you carry it off."

Jessica looked for a long minute at the imperious, splendid beauty of Lady Maria Selsey. For the first time in this interview she smiled. "I am quite sure you could carry off anything," she said. "Even me."

The haughtiness vanished from Maria's face, and she grinned. "I don't like to boast, Jessica, but I do wield a great deal of influence. Set your mind at rest. If I say you will be accepted, you will be." She rose to her feet. "Philip is waiting in the library and I'm sure he has paced a hole in the carpet by now. Shall I go and send him to you?"

Wild roses flew in Jessica's cheeks. "Please," she said breathlessly.

Maria left and after what seemed an eternity the

door opened again and he was there. "Jess?" he said, and with a small cry she ran across the room and into his arms.

Half an hour later Maria returned, knocking discreetly on the door before she entered. Jessica and Linton were seated side by side on the sofa. Jessica's eyes looked like stars and Linton's hair was disordered. He grinned at Maria. "You are a pearl among sisters, my dear," he said, rising and setting a chair for her.

She looked into the blue of his eyes and heaved a little sigh of relief. It was all right. She smiled mischievously. "I am having a marvelous time," she declared. "And did you remember to give Jessica mother's letter?"

"He did," Jessica replied softly. "It was very kind. She wants us to be married at Staplehurst."

"I don't care where we are married so long as it is soon," said Linton decidedly.

The stars in Jessica's eyes dimmed. "Philip," she said in a low, muted voice, "what am I going to to tell the boys?"

"I have been thinking about that," he replied, turning to look down into her anxious face. "I assume they will make their home with us at Staplehurst?"

Jessica bit her lip. "They'll have to."

"Yes, they will. For a few years at least. Jess," he picked up her hand and looked down at it intently. "What do you want to do about Winchcombe?"

There was silence as she sat thinking, then he felt

her hand stiffen in his. "Philip," she said excitedly, "I'll give Winchcombe to Geoffrey!"

He kept his eyes on her hand. "Are you sure?"

"Yes. He loves it. It's part of him. And it will enable him to have a financially secure future. Adrian will be a doctor. He's wanted nothing else ever since he was a small boy. But for Geoffrey it's Winchcombe—and horses."

"He sounds exactly like my Matthew," said Maria resignedly. "I suppose that's why they're such great friends."

"Well, that's settled, then," Linton said briskly. "You tell the boys that you are going to marry me and move the family to Staplehurst but that we will continue the stud here at Winchcombe. We can plan to spend a part of their holidays here each year and I'll hire someone to be here at the stables full time, supervising. In fact I have someone in mind. By the time Geoffrey is ready to take over in a few years the place should be established."

Jessica had been watching him steadily all through this speech, and now she said, a hint of accusation in her voice, "You had all this planned out already."

A smile glinted in the blue of his eyes. "It does seem the practical solution."

The corners of her mouth deepened, and she went on looking at him. "You tell the boys you are going to marry me, my darling," he said gently. "Tell them about your plans for Winchcombe. Let me tell them the rest."

Jessica's throat was dry. "I suppose they have to know?"

209

"They have to know something," he said reasonably. "Leave it to me to handle."

"All right," said Jessica, deeply thankful that that was a task she did not have to tackle. It would be bad enough telling Miss Burnley.

They had a celebration dinner at Winchcombe that evening. Whatever Linton had told the boys had left them a trifle awed and respectful of Jessica, a state of affairs that had lasted all of forty-five minutes. By the time they sat down to dinner their usual youthful spirits had been restored. The security of their young lives had been threatened by financial problems ever since the death of their father. They had also been upset by the prolonged absence of their sister and then by her preoccupation when she finally returned. It felt comfortable sitting at the table with this big, fair-haired man who looked at them with interest and who was obviously competent to deal with any problems that might arise to plague them in the future. Geoffrey was happy because he was to have Winchcombe and because he would be living near his greatest friend, whose mother had already invited him on a visit. Adrian, more of a child, was content because his sister looked happy and now he was sure she would not go away again.

Miss Burnley, too, was relieved to know that she would be staying at Winchcombe, although she still had not gotten over the shock of Jessica's revelation that afternoon. That Jessica should become an actress was bad enough, but the other. . . . Even now Miss Burnley's mind shied away from the awful truth. Her eyes went once again to the Earl of Linton who, miraculously to Miss Burnley, wanted to marry Jessica, even after . . .

Linton had been listening to Adrian and, as Miss Burnley watched, his eyes, warm with laughter, turned to Jessica. She was talking to Lady Maria and for a moment Miss Burnley, too, watched that unconscious, serious face.

It had always been a serious face, Miss Burnley reflected. Too serious for so young a girl. But then Jessica had had burdens foreign to most young girls of her age and class. They had been responsibilities she had uncomplainingly taken on her slender shoulders, but if she had not protested, that did not mean they were any the less heavy. She had run Winchcombe for years, watching helplessly as her inheritance was steadily milked of everything that had once made it prosperous. She had virtually reared two small boys by herself. And then, after working like a laborer for over a year, she had faced the prospect of losing everything to a man she distrusted and despised.

Jessica's head turned, and her eyes met Linton's. They looked at each other for a minute, then he turned away to answer something Geoffrey had said to him and Jessica went back to her conversation with Lady Maria. Miss Burnley bent her head and stared at her plate.

It had sounded sordid, Jessica's revelation to Miss Burnley this afternoon. But who was she to judge Jessica, Miss Burnley thought now humbly, as she gazed fixedly at her peas. The very food on her plate, the roof over her head, were there because of Jessica.

*She* had never had to make the kind of decision Jessica had. She had always been protected by the very girl whose conduct she had been silently condemning.

She had been shocked at Jessica's revelation, but she had been almost equally shocked to find that, instead of being punished, Jessica was actually going to benefit from her misdeed. The wages of Jessica's sin was marriage with one of the richest nobles in the country.

Instead of her peas Miss Burnley saw once again the too thin face of her former pupil. She remembered the withdrawn, sleepwalker's expression that face had worn during these past months. If Jessica had sinned she had suffered as well. And if her future looked bright now—well, no one deserved it more, Miss Burnley thought fiercely.

"Burnie!" It was Jessica's voice, lightly teasing. "Have you gone off into a trance?"

"No, my dear." Miss Burnley looked at the glowing face on her right. "I have been thinking about you."

"About me. Oh." Jessica's voice was ever so slightly defensive.

"Yes," said Miss Burnley clearly. "I have been wondering if Lord Linton realizes how very fortunate he is."

There was a moment of surprised silence; then Jessica smiled, a radiant, youthful smile. "Thank you, Burnie," she said.

"Why is Philip fortunate?" asked Adrian, his inquisitive eyes on his sister and governess.

"Because your sister has done me the honor of accepting my offer of marriage," Linton replied promptly.

"Oh, that," said Adrian. He helped himself to more peas and then, apparently feeling that more of a response was called for, he added kindly, "It's true, you know. There's no one like Jess."

For the second time during the meal Linton's eyes found hers. "I know that, Adrian," he said softly.

"Jess!" said Geoffrey urgently. "If we brought Northern Light to Staplehurst, do you think you could go on working him?"

"No, Geoffrey," Linton said with great firmness. "We will engage adequate staff to fulfill all your instructions. Your sister is going out of the horse-training business. Permanently."

"Goodness," Jessica said to Lady Maria, laughter in her eyes. "Is he always so autocratic?"

"Yes," Maria said decisively. "He may have a smile that melts stones but in his heart of hearts, Philip is a despot."

They all looked from Lady Maria to the blue-eyed man sitting at the head of the table. "But I'm very kind to women and children," he said serenely. He smiled. "May I have some more peas?"

Jessica smiled back. "Certainly you may. Pass Philip the peas, Adrian."

Adrian hastened to obey, and Geoffrey said, "If you aren't going to train horses, Jess, what *are* you going to do?"

Jessica tilted her head reflectively. "I am not quite sure, Geoffrey," she said at last with wide-eyed solemnity. "Perhaps Philip will be able to think of something."

"I'll try," he assured her, his eyes glinting between narrowed lids. "I'm sure I can find something to keep you busy."

Lady Maria, who felt the conversation was entering dangerous waters, firmly changed the subject, and Jessica obligingly followed her lead. Linton calmly went on eating his peas.

## About the Author

Joan Wolf is a native of New York City who presently resides in Milford, Connecticut, with her husband and two young children. She taught high school English in New York for nine years and took up writing when she retired to rear a family. Her previous books, THE COUNTERFEIT MARRIAGE, A KIND OF HONOR, A LONDON SEASON, A DIFFICULT TRUCE, and THE SCOTTISH LORD, are also available in Signet editions.

## More Regency Romances from SIGNET